"I'd like to see you, Maria.

"You can bring Sam, if you like. Maybe you could show me some of the sights, and I could buy you dinner."

"I don't date." She gave Joe the standard answer she'd used many times. Her hands were trembling. She didn't look at Joe as she spoke. She was afraid he might see the yearning that welled up in her suddenly at the idea of spending time with him. It might have been dark, but her imagination made that desire feel like a hot, golden glow inside her.

Joe touched her clasped hands, and suddenly the nights were too long and the years ahead stared back at her. "You're shaking," he observed softly. "Scared or cold?"

"Scared," she admitted softly. Looking at Joe in the dim light, she knew he wasn't the right one. She couldn't get involved with Joe. She couldn't get involved with *any* lawman.

Dear Reader,

Happy Valentine's Day! What better way to celebrate than with a Silhouette Romance novel? We're sweeter than chocolate—and less damaging to the hips! This month is filled with special treats just for you. LOVING THE BOSS, our six-book series about office romances that lead to happily ever after, continues with *The Night Before Baby* by Karen Rose Smith. In this sparkling story, an unforgettable one-night stand—during the company Christmas party!—leads to an unexpected pregnancy and a must-read marriage of convenience.

Teresa Southwick crafts an emotional BUNDLES OF JOY title, in which the forbidden man of her dreams becomes a pregnant woman's stand-in groom. Don't miss *A Vow, a Ring, a Baby Swing*. When a devil-may-care bachelor discovers he's a daddy, he offers the prim heroine a chance to hold a *Baby in Her Arms*, as Judy Christenberry's LUCKY CHARM SISTERS trilogy resumes.

Award-winning author Marie Ferrarella proves it's *Never Too Late for Love* as the bride's mother and the groom's widower father discover their children's wedding was just the beginning in this charming continuation of LIKE MOTHER, LIKE DAUGHTER. Beloved author Arlene James lends a traditional touch to Silhouette Romance's ongoing HE'S MY HERO promotion with *Mr. Right Next Door*. And FAMILY MATTERS spotlights new talent Elyssa Henry with her heartwarming debut, *A Family for the Sheriff*.

Treat yourself to each and every offering this month. And in future months, look for more of the stories you love…and the authors you cherish.

Enjoy!

Mary-Theresa Hussey

Mary-Theresa Hussey
Senior Editor, Silhouette Romance

Please address questions and book requests to:
Silhouette Reader Service
U.S.: 3010 Walden Ave., P.O. Box 1325, Buffalo, NY 14269
Canadian: P.O. Box 609, Fort Erie, Ont. L2A 5X3

A FAMILY FOR THE SHERIFF

Elyssa Henry

Silhouette

R O M A N C E™

Published by Silhouette Books

America's Publisher of Contemporary Romance

For my mother,
who told me to dream big,
and Cathleen Treacy, my editor,
who helped me get there

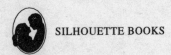 SILHOUETTE BOOKS

ISBN 0-373-19353-X

A FAMILY FOR THE SHERIFF

Copyright © 1999 by Joyce Lavene

This edition published by arrangement with Harlequin Books S.A.

® and TM are trademarks of Harlequin Books S.A., used under license.
Trademarks indicated with ® are registered in the United States Patent
and Trademark Office, the Canadian Trade Marks Office and in other
countries.

Printed in U.S.A.

ELYSSA HENRY

is the pseudonym of Joyce and James Lavene, a married writing team with over twenty-five years of experience in romance. They share their time with three children and one grandchild. When they aren't writing, they prowl the roads looking for adventure and the next story that has to be told.

Dear Reader,

We've all experienced the loss of a loved one. The heartbreak and loneliness can only be healed by time and patience. The journey continues for those of us left behind, and our lives are changed forever.

Being part of a family is a lifelong bond. Our relationships with those we love give us strength and acceptance as we face the world. Even when a fragile thread of that link is broken, our memories sustain us. As a family, we gather closer, and we hold each other tightly.

And sometimes, a very special person happens our way, and, as a family, we embrace them. Learning to live and trust again, as Maria and Joe do, can be a challenge. Yet creating a new life, forged with love and understanding, is how families are born. We sigh a little for the past, then we move on, with hope, to the future.

Wishing all the best to you and your loved ones,

Elyssa Henry

Chapter One

Maria sighed and stopped the truck.

It had been raining steadily for the past three days, making the landscape look like a French watercolor. Water washed in waves across the cracked window of the pickup truck she drove, and the worn windshield wipers did little to clear the glass.

It was the way he walked that stopped her. Rain ran in rivers down his jacket, his jeans already dark with it. His shoulders were hunched against the onslaught, and he waded through ankle-deep water at the side of the road.

Still, he wasn't hitchhiking. She couldn't be sure he needed or wanted a ride. He walked steadily, long legs eating up the distance. There was purpose in his stride.

But they were on a stretch of road that ran through ten miles of jack pine and very little else. The only spot there was a phone, or any type of human environment, was five miles away in Gold Springs, where she was headed.

She backed up carefully, the old truck shuddering, protesting the abuse. She rolled down the window, wondering what she was going to say, hoping he wouldn't get the wrong idea. Hoping she wasn't crazy for offering a stranger a ride on a deserted stretch of highway.

"Want a ride?" she yelled past the steady pounding of the rain.

"Yeah, thanks," he replied simply. He grabbed hold of the door handle and opened the door.

When he swung his long form into the cab, closing the door quickly behind him, she had her first sense of panic.

He was bigger than she'd thought when she'd first seen him, and he looked tough.

"Sorry to get your seat wet," he said as he rolled up the window. "My name's Roberts—"

He held out his hand as she held up her tire iron, facing him squarely across the seat.

She didn't know what she'd expected. Maybe shock, maybe anger, but there was only a mild amusement in his dark eyes.

His face was wet, water dripping from his hair and sun-darkened skin. He looked as though he lived outside. Black hair was slicked back from his high forehead by a careless hand, and his mouth was destined for laughter.

"Joe Roberts," he concluded, not lowering his hand. His eyes locked on hers. "And I'll be happy to get out the same way I came in if it'll make you feel any better."

"I just wanted you to know that I may be alone but I'm not helpless," she replied evenly, holding the tire iron in both gloved hands.

"I appreciate that, ma'am." He nodded slightly. "I was hoping you weren't going to mug me."

"I, uh—" She paused and cleared her throat then put the tire iron down beside the seat. "I've just never picked a man up before." Her eyes flew across to his as she realized what she had said. "I mean, given a stranger a ride."

"I guessed as much. You probably don't have any business doing it now. But I appreciate it."

"Maria Lightner." She put her hand into his, feeling foolish. "I'm going to Gold Springs. It's just up the road. I thought you could use a lift to a phone or something."

"As a matter of fact," he replied as she put the truck into gear, "I'm on my way to Gold Springs. My car broke down about three miles back."

She glanced at him again. Historians spent time in Gold Springs, but he didn't look like a historian. Yet, there was something familiar about his name. She was sure he wasn't a local. Maria had lived in the small town since she'd been born. She knew everyone and their children and grandchildren.

"You could have Billy come out for your car," she told him, still trying to identify his name. "He owns the only repair shop in town."

"That'd be great," he answered. "What about you? What do you do in Gold Springs?"

"I own a small farm, nothing major, just a few acres," she replied, keeping her eyes on the wet road with great difficulty. His gaze hadn't moved from her face since she'd started driving. It was unnerving.

"I would've never thought of you being a farmer," he told her, leaning back against the truck door. "You remind me more of a teacher."

"A teacher?" She laughed. "I hated school."

"So did my sister, but she teaches now. Third grade. I keep imagining her in the middle of thirty kids. She didn't even like to baby-sit."

"I'm afraid I don't do anything so important." She shook her head. "I raise herbs and keep a few bees."

"Really?" He shuddered. "I can't imagine that. Being a city boy, bugs make me a little shaky."

"They take some getting used to," she acknowledged, "but then so would a classroom of thirty eight-year-olds."

He agreed with a laugh. "I think I could get used to the bugs first."

The windshield wipers slapped together in the silence for a moment, then Maria had to ask.

"So, are you planning to stay in Gold Springs?" she wondered. It was rare for anyone who wasn't from there to come to live in the old mining town. "Do you have relatives there?"

"No." He smiled. "My family's scattered everywhere in the world except here. I'm starting the new sheriff's office in Gold Springs. The job came with a house and some land. I think I'm going to be settling down here."

"What?" She couldn't believe his words. "You're Joseph Roberts? From Chicago?"

"Originally." He shrugged. "I guess it's true what they say about small towns. News travels fast."

Maria felt her fingers tighten on the old steering wheel. "You don't know the half of it."

She pulled the truck into the parking lot of the old general store, the first place to stop after the small sign that announced the whereabouts of Gold Springs.

"There's a phone in there," she told him, seeing the

interested eyes looking out the store window as he opened the truck door.

"Thanks." He nodded and started to climb out. "Maybe I'll see you around."

"Goodbye, Mr. Roberts," she said firmly. As soon as the truck door was closed, she pushed the truck into gear and sped out of the parking lot.

Of all the people to have picked up on the road! Joe Roberts didn't know it, but he was going to have one hell of a time living in Gold Springs! No one wanted him there, and everyone was prepared to tell him.

It was a vain hope, she knew, that no one would recognize her pickup in the rain. When she ran into the house after parking the truck, the phone was already ringing.

"What the hell were you doing?" Tommy Lightner demanded with no preliminary. "You brought Joe Roberts here knowing the way everyone feels? I thought you were with us, Maria?"

"I'm not with anyone." She shook her head, water droplets flying around her as she put her groceries down and took off her gloves. "I've never said that, Tommy."

"So you're against us?" he asked hotly.

She let out a long breath. "No, I'm not against you, and I agree, the commissioners should have asked us before they hired him. But trying to take it out on this man is wrong, and everyone knows it. As for giving him a ride, his car had broken down. I didn't know who he was."

He was nearly speechless. "You gave a complete stranger a ride?"

"It was raining. I stopped and gave him a ride for the last few miles into town. I didn't know who he was at the time, but I would have given him a ride anyway, Tommy. He's still a human being.''

"A human being we don't want here," Tommy raged. "Are you forgetting Josh already? Josh would have been sheriff if he hadn't been killed. Doesn't that mean anything to you?''

"I have to go, Tommy," she mumbled wearily into the mouthpiece. "Sam's due home soon. I'll talk to you later."

She hung up, not giving him a chance to say anything they both might regret later. He was her brother-in-law and Sam's uncle. She didn't want to alienate him.

She bustled around the kitchen, stowing away bottles and cans until she paused to look out the big window above the sink.

Josh had loved that window, that view of the rolling, green hills that made up their land. Just hearing his name still hurt, but that didn't make it right to take it out on Joe Roberts. He was only doing his job. The county had paid him to come to Gold Springs.

The town had been in need of a sheriff's department away from the county police force that cruised by when there was trouble. The rapid encroachment of the outlying housing developments was making its formation even more important.

Gold Springs was growing. The people needed the stability a full-time sheriff's department would bring to the area.

But everyone resented the fact that they hadn't chosen another man from town to head the project after Josh had died.

Josh Lightner had been the town constable for ten years after old Mike Matthews had retired. When Josh was gone, Mike Matthews had agreed to step into the role, but only until they could find someone to replace him.

Tommy Lightner had been deputy to both men, and everyone had expected the county commission to name him as the new sheriff. But they had done an about-face and hired someone with experience from outside the area.

"Mom, Mom!" Her son burst into the kitchen, the door slamming against the wall with his exuberance. "Guess what happened? My science project won second place."

He held up the red ribbon proudly and grinned at her, the sight of several missing teeth in the front of his mouth tugging at her heartstrings.

Sam was the image of his father. Light brown hair, big blue eyes. Even the scattering of freckles on his nose and the tiny dimple in his cheek.

Thinking of Josh, of all the things he would miss, brought tears to her eyes as she knelt and hugged Sam to her.

"That's wonderful," she told him. "After all the hard work we put into it, I'm glad it paid off."

"Don't cry, Mom." He touched her cheek with his dirty hand. "It was just a science project."

"I know," she answered, her voice husky despite her efforts to control it. "And I'm not really crying."

But they both knew better. Sam was only eight, but he had seen his mother cry too many times since his father's death to be misled.

He hugged her tightly. "I love you, Mom."

"I love you, too, Sam." She hugged him again, then collected herself, stood up and took his heavy book bag and lunch box from him. "And I think we should go

out and celebrate tonight. What do you think about
Pizza Express?''

"Cool!" he said. "Can I get tokens to play the
games, too?''

"I think so," she agreed. "Put your stuff away and
we'll go. It's supposed to rain all night again, and I'd
like to be back before it gets late.''

He smirked. "Oh, Mom! You think late is seven or
eight. People stay out until ten sometimes, you know.''

"Not people who have to go to school tomorrow,''
she retorted, putting on her coat while he ran up the
stairs to his bedroom.

Maria wiped her cheeks with an impatient hand. As
often as she promised herself that she wouldn't cry
anymore, it still caught her by surprise from time to
time.

It wasn't like it could bring him back. Josh and their
life together were gone. No wailing or sighing could
change that fact. Yet she still cried for him sometimes
in the night when the waste of his life choked up inside
of her.

The rain had let up as Maria and Sam went out to
start up the old truck. They didn't go into the town of
Rockford often. A good thing, she mused, since she
didn't know how many miles the truck had left to go
on its life.

"We need a new truck," Sam told her as the truck
putt-putted down the driveway. "Ronnie's father just
got a new one.''

"I know," she said, looking over her shoulder until
they were clear of the drainage ditch on either side of
the road.

"Uncle Tommy said he could get you a new one,''
Sam informed her innocently.

Maria grimaced in the rearview mirror. Blue eyes reflected the information back to her that she couldn't tell her son, that his uncle had made the same offer to her under different circumstances. And she hadn't liked the strings that were attached.

"We get along fine with what we have," she replied calmly, pushing a strand of reddish brown hair from her cheek.

"We could get along better with a new truck," Sam responded, looking out the window at the passing landscape.

"You're sounding more like your father every day." She shook her head, then glanced at him. "Stubborn like him, too."

He nodded solemnly. "Thanks. Everyone knows my dad was a great guy. He was a hero."

"So he was," she whispered through a tight throat. She looked up quickly when a solitary figure came into view as they were passing the general store on the way out of Gold Springs going toward Rockford.

"Hitchhiker," Sam said, identifying the man.

"Not exactly," Maria said, drawing in a deep breath as she made her decision before they reached him.

"What are you doing? Mom? Are we picking up a hitchhiker?"

"You watch too much television, Sam," she countered, slowing down. "Scoot over here and be quiet a minute."

Sam stared at her but he did as he was told, pushing away from the door and hugging her side.

"Need a lift somewhere?" she offered, her heart pounding in her throat as Joe opened the cab door.

He took in the addition to the truck's passengers and

ended up with his dark eyes locked on hers. "I think you know the answer to that."

There was no laughter in that gaze, she noticed. She had the grace to look at her hands briefly. He was angry, and she didn't blame him. The county commissioners had put them all in a bad place.

"Get in and I'll take you into town," she offered, knowing she was asking for trouble. It just seemed like the least she could do.

Joe climbed into the cab and pulled the door closed. Her light perfume curled around him invitingly. He felt her eyes on him as he fastened his seat belt and he fumbled with the clasp. When he looked up, her gaze slid away. There was no mistaking that the boy was hers. The big, soulful blue eyes fastened on him in a way the woman's wouldn't have, but they were identical.

A pang of regret shivered through him. A different turn, another road. The boy could have been his son. He shrugged it off. Regret was something he had lived with for a long time.

"Billy wouldn't bring in your car," she guessed, starting down the road, turning on the windshield wipers as the rain began again.

"I would've had to use the phone to find out," he replied tautly. "Since all the phone lines were down in the entire town and I don't know where to find the repair shop..."

"The phones were working," Sam volunteered quickly. "Mr. Maddox, the bus driver, stopped off and called home after we turned past the store."

"I guess there was some mistake." Maria grimaced at her son.

"I guess so." Joe stared out the window. "A big mistake."

Maria concentrated on her driving, trying not to think about what she was doing. They were nearly to Rockford before they passed a blur of red through the rain-coated windows.

"Is that your car?" Sam asked eagerly.

"That's it."

"What's wrong with it?"

"Sam." Maria tried to hush her son's curiosity.

"It's all right," Joe told her, glancing at her taut face over her son's head. "It's not his fault."

Maria kept her eyes stubbornly on the road as he explained that he had forgotten to pack another spare tire after the first one had blown out about a hundred miles away.

"That was pretty careless," Sam remarked, eyeing the stranger warily.

"It was," Joe replied steadily, then smiled at him. "Very careless."

"What kind of car was that?" Sam asked. "I think I saw one like it in a magazine."

"It's a Porsche," he told the boy. "It'll do a hundred and sixty down a straightaway like this."

"Wow! Can I have a ride sometime?" Sam looked at him in a new light. Anyone who had a car like that couldn't be all bad.

"Not when it's going a hundred and sixty down a straightaway," Maria told him bluntly, stopping at the first red light at the edge of Rockford.

She looked at Joe Roberts in the fading daylight, wondering why on earth she had stopped to help him again. She didn't know anything about him except that he was qualified to run a sheriff's department.

And that she felt sorry for him. He hadn't seen the house the commission had promised him yet.

"I'm trading it in, anyway," Joe told him. "Just as soon as I replace the tire."

"Why?" Sam demanded.

"I think I'm going to need something a little different now," Joe replied thoughtfully. "Maybe something more like this truck."

"You can have this one," Sam offered. "Maybe you could buy it from Mom and then she could afford to get a new one."

Maria stepped on the gas, feeling annoyance warm her face. There was no such thing as a tactful eight-year-old.

Joe laughed. "I have a younger sister," he told her in a low voice. "My mother made me take her out on dates with me so I wouldn't get into trouble. Trust me. This is nothing."

Sam rambled on about his science fair project, describing in detail how the mosquito larvae hatched into mosquitoes. He explained that they were on their way out to dinner because of his second-place award and that he would be happy to show the project and the award to Joe sometime.

"I'd like to see it," Joe assured him. "Any place is fine," he told Maria as they cruised down the crowded city streets.

"I know a place right next door to where we're going," she told him, wondering if her knuckles were turning white with the pressure she was exerting on the steering wheel. "You could get your tire there, and we could run you out with it on the way home."

"That's way too much," Joe said. "The ride in is fine."

"It's no trouble," she lied. She wasn't sure it wasn't going to be more trouble than it was worth. Still, she felt obligated to help him.

The commission had brought him a long way and promised him a good job. Tommy and his family wouldn't let him stay, no matter what it took to convince him. He was a stranger, but anyone deserved better.

"I appreciate it." He tried to see her face, but the light was gone. She had to be going out on a limb, and he couldn't figure out why. "I'd like to buy your pizza, if that's okay."

"Great!" Sam said happily. "That's more coins for the games!"

"Wait a sec," Joe said. "This isn't one of those gizmo games and pizza places, is it? I hate those places."

"There's a few games," Sam said defensively. "They're in another room."

"That's not it," Joe answered as they opened the truck doors to get out. "They know me at all of them. I'm the best, you know."

Sam stared at him with newfound awe for an instant then rolled his eyes. "Get out of here! I could take you on at any of the jumping games. Nobody beats me at those."

"I'm sorry," Joe told him mournfully. "Maybe I shouldn't go in with you—"

"I don't believe it." Sam laughed, sliding across the seat to jump down. "You can't be that good. Nobody's that good."

Joe shook his head and stared at the ground. "Well, anyway, your mom hasn't said—"

"Mom." Sam turned to Maria, who'd been about to

give his offer a flat thanks, but no thanks. "We have to let him go with us. I know he's lying."

Maria glanced at Joe's dark eyes fixed on her son's back, a slight smile tugging at the corners of his mouth.

She sighed, hoping they wouldn't run into anyone they knew. "He can come with us. Can we get out of the rain now?"

It was crowded for a Wednesday night. Maria winced at every voice, worrying that someone she knew would be there. No one from Gold Springs would understand her helping Joe Roberts.

She wasn't sure she understood it herself.

They found a table and ordered pizza, then Joe and Sam disappeared into the game room. The music was loud, and the excited screams from the game room punctuated the laughter and the calls for pickup in the pizza kitchen.

Costumed characters posed for pictures with their arms around children and adults alike. Flashing lights danced in time to the music while a group of waiters sang "Happy Birthday" slightly off tune.

Maria put a hand to her head. It was beginning to ache. Her life wasn't usually more stressful than trying to get a good price from her herb crop. A chance encounter had made her placid existence choppy.

It wasn't that she was afraid of her neighbors and family. She just didn't want them to think she didn't support them. It wasn't in her nature to thrive on controversy.

"Wow!" Sam jumped into his chair at her side, his face flushed but happy. "He's good."

Joe took the chair opposite and grinned at him across the table. "I've spent so much time in places where there wasn't anything else to do.'' He shrugged. ''That's why I'm the best.''

''He might be.'' Sam grinned then jumped up. ''Can I go back and try Wrangler again?''

''Go ahead,'' Maria told him. ''The pizzas haven't even gone in yet.''

''Thanks.'' He took a few more coins from her. ''If I keep practicing, I could be as good as Joe. He said I have natural talent.''

Maria smiled and glanced at Joe. ''That's great. Good luck.''

''Call me if the pizza comes,'' he yelled as he was running away.

Maria faced the man across the gleaming white table. ''I'm not sure I should thank you for telling him to practice.''

''Definitely not.'' He shook his head, resting his arms on the table. ''I wanted some time to talk to you alone. It seemed the easiest way.''

Maria tensed, looking at a napkin she had neatly folded on the table.

''Look, I'm sorry about what's happened,'' she said. ''It got out of hand.''

''What exactly has happened?'' he asked, leaning forward, trying to catch her eye. ''Surely I have the right to know that, anyway.''

''It's not easy to explain.'' She unfolded the white paper napkin. ''The county commission and the town disagreed about who should run the new sheriff's department. It sounds silly, I know, but the town felt like it should be someone from Gold Springs. Someone who knows the area.''

''They told me that there wasn't anyone who knew

enough to set up the type of department they wanted,''
Joe explained.

"The Lightners are the biggest problem.'' She bit
her lip, feeling as though she was somehow betraying
Tommy and the others.

"Your husband?'' he wondered.

Her eyes met his then, and the depth of sorrow he
saw there made him sorry he had wanted to know the
truth.

"My brother-in-law. My husband died two years
ago. He was Gold Springs' constable. He might have
been the new sheriff.''

"I'm sorry.'' He felt trite when the words were out
of his mouth. "This must be hard for you.''

She looked up again, her hair falling back a little
from her face. "Actually, it's not like that for me. It
seems to hurt the others, Tommy and Josh's parents,
more than me. Maybe that's because I always hated
Josh doing that job. It's what killed him.''

Joe drew a deep breath and looked away for an instant, not relishing the memories those words dredged
up for him. "So it's nothing personal. They would have
hated anyone.''

"That's true,'' she agreed with a shrug. "Only
Tommy would have been good enough for the Lightners once Josh was gone.''

"Why didn't Tommy get the training and take the
job?'' he asked, his voice harsh.

Maria smiled. "The commission made it clear from
the beginning that they wanted someone with experience in setting up a sheriff's department. Even if he'd
had the training, Tommy would have been out of his
depth. Josh had law enforcement training. They would
have worked with him.''

Maria looked at the paper napkin only to find that she had shredded it.

Joe touched her hand lightly, stopping its restless destruction, then jerked his fingers away as though he'd been burned.

"I'm sorry to cause you this trouble. There wasn't any way for me to know."

"There wasn't," she agreed, picking up the pieces of napkin and depositing them in a trash container near their table. "I'm sorry for you, too." She took her seat again and looked at him more thoroughly in the bright lights.

He had a kind face, she thought, and eyes that did understand what she was feeling, because he looked as though he had been hurt a few times himself. And there was something more. Something she'd never expected to feel again. Something she thought had died with her husband. Heat. Fire. When Joe touched her; when he looked at her. She didn't want to feel that way but she couldn't deny it. His voice seemed to hold her, stroke her. His words shivered down her spine.

"Don't be." He smiled, his eyes glittering as he made a rapid decision. He wasn't running anymore. From his memories or this place. "I don't plan on going anywhere."

"Maybe you don't understand—"

The pizza arrived, accompanied by Sam's loud whoops of excitement.

"Look who's here, Mom." He dragged his tow-headed friend to the table. "Ronnie's science project won first prize, and his dad brought him here, too."

"Dad says we should share a table," Ronnie said in a voice that said he didn't care as long as he could get back to the games. "He's right over there."

Maria looked across the crowded restaurant, and Ronnie's father, Ron, waved to her enthusiastically. He pointed at the empty seats at his table and motioned for her to join him.

"Oh, God," she moaned. "I can't believe it."

"They better get used to the idea." Joe waved and flashed a smile. "I guess it might as well be now."

"I have to live here," she told him. "Everyone's going to think I planned this."

"I'm sorry, Maria," he assured her quietly. "I didn't plan this, either."

"Maria!" Ron approached their table, a pitcher of soda in his hand. "I think my table was bigger, darlin', but if you'd rather sit down here, that's fine with me." He pulled two chairs to their table.

Maria glared at Joe, who looked the other way. Is this what she deserved for her good deed? She should have kept herself out of it. Then she wouldn't be sitting here waiting for the fat to hit the fire.

"I don't believe we've met." Ron hitched up his pants and stuck out his hand to the stranger across the table. "Ron Washington."

"Joe Roberts." Joe took his hand in a hard grip. His gaze targeted the other man's as Ron's face went from friendly to hostile.

"Joe Roberts?" Ron spluttered, staring at Maria, who wouldn't look at him. "From Chicago?"

"Yeah." Joe grinned. "How 'bout those Cubs?"

Chapter Two

"Why is he here?" Ron demanded when Sam came and pulled Joe off to the game room after they had finished eating.

"You know why he's here," Maria returned angrily.

"You know what I mean! He should have been in that fancy car of his and gone already. I never expected to actually meet him! Especially not here with you!"

"Ron, it doesn't matter to me if someone else does Josh's job. Especially a stranger. I've already had enough of that. So you and Tommy will just have to fight your own battles."

Ron was thrown off guard by Maria's outburst. He was a small, mean man who gloried in any sense of power. His dark hair was thick and greasy, slicked back from his forehead.

"Maria, honey." His tone was clearly conciliatory. "I know Josh's death has been hard for you and the boy, but...you aren't dating the man, are you?"

"No." Maria ground the word out, pushing her last

bite of pizza aside. "But it wouldn't have anything to do with you if I was dating him. He plans on staying, Ron, and after meeting him, I don't think there's anything anyone can do to change his mind."

"He hasn't seen the house yet." He grinned and wiggled his eyebrows. "After that, we'll just see, won't we?"

"I think you might be surprised," she informed him darkly. She wasn't sure what they had expected, but she didn't think they were prepared for Joe Roberts.

Ron left her, headed for the game room, found his son and led him out of the restaurant.

Maria's headache had turned vicious halfway through the meal. She'd searched her purse for an aspirin but had come up empty.

It wasn't anything that had been said between the two men. Ronnie had behaved as though Joe was a long-lost cousin. He didn't have enough nerve to tackle the taller, clearly better conditioned man by himself.

But his glances at Maria had told her that it was far from over. He would head to Gold Springs and be on the phone all night telling everyone what had happened at the pizza restaurant.

Joe had tried to talk to Ronnie about the changes that were coming, about the needs the county felt weren't being met with the present arrangement.

Ron nodded and didn't say anything, preferring to keep his vehemence until Joe had left them alone at the table. Then he had lashed out at Maria, leaving nothing unsaid.

"Is everything all right?" Joe asked, bringing Sam back with him after Ronnie had gone.

Maria looked at him, her head pounding. "All

right?'' she asked scornfully. ''No, everything isn't all right!''

''Maybe we should leave,'' Joe suggested, and Sam nodded.

''She gets upset sometimes,'' he told the older man.

''Sometimes, women take things the wrong way,'' Joe returned with a sigh.

''I think we should leave right now.'' Maria glared at them both and stuck the check for the pizza in Joe's hand. ''Thanks for supper.''

She stormed past Joe and took Sam's hand in a firm grip as she pushed open the door into the cool, rainy night.

''Aren't we waiting for him like you said?'' Sam asked as she headed for the truck. ''We can't just leave him,'' he continued when she didn't answer.

Behind the wheel of the truck, Maria contemplated doing just that. Helping Joe Roberts wasn't going to be worth the hell she would go through every time she came in contact with someone from town.

And he had certainly left her out to dry by announcing who he was to Ron. She had explained the situation to him. He could have kept it to himself. He could have—

''Mom?'' Sam tried to get her attention as Joe walked out of the tire store with a new tire on his arm. ''Are we going to let him walk out to his car after you promised him a ride?''

Maria could hear by the tone in her son's voice that leaving Joe would be an unforgivable event.

She sighed and started up the truck. ''We'll give him a ride out there, Sam. But then we won't see him anymore, okay?''

"Okay, I guess. But I don't understand why we can't see him."

Maria knew she had only herself to blame. She should have left well enough alone. There was no way the town would ever accept Joe Roberts as sheriff. Trying to be nice was only prolonging the inevitable.

But she'd finish what she started. She pulled the truck into the tire store parking lot and waited while Sam opened the truck door.

"He can put the tire in the back, can't he, Mom?" Sam turned to her.

"Sure," she answered curtly.

She didn't look at Joe as he closed the truck door behind him. Nothing that had happened was his fault. She had put herself in an awkward position by picking him up in the first place.

But she was mad anyway. He seemed like a decent person, but there was no way to win this fight. The best he could do was to change his tire and go on with his life.

Joe and Sam kept a quick-paced conversation going while the truck took them out of town. They talked about games and science, wondering about virtual reality, a favorite concept of Sam's.

"You have a computer with a CD ROM?" Sam whistled. "I'd really like to see that."

"Anytime," Joe promised easily.

Maria seethed and tried to coax a little more speed out of the old truck. She didn't like to think of Sam being let down, but once they let him off at his car, they wouldn't be seeing Joe Roberts again.

She let out a sigh of relief when she saw the exotic red car in the headlight beams.

"Here we are," she said, pulling the truck up behind the car on the shoulder.

"I appreciate this," Joe said, climbing out of the truck. "I know it won't be easy for you to explain."

"I can take care of it," she announced stiffly, wishing he would go.

"Can't we wait until the tire is fixed and I can ride back with him?" Sam interrupted.

"I don't think—"

"I'd like that." Joe agreed hopefully. "It shouldn't take long."

"Sam," Maria groaned. "You're not riding in that car."

"Mom! He said himself he's trading it! It might be the last chance I have to ride in a car like that!"

"No, Sam," she said.

"It's no problem," Joe assured her. "And I promise to go the speed limit."

"Please, Mom!"

"I'll just be out here changing this tire." Joe backed out of the argument.

"Mom!" Sam pleaded. "We're just a few miles from home, and you'll be behind us. Can't I go with him? Just this once?"

Maria decided later that her headache had brought about insanity and that was why she'd agreed to the request. Nothing else could account for it.

"All right." She shook her head. "All right. You can ride home with him and then you can get in the shower and go to bed."

"Yes, ma'am!" Sam whooped and jumped out of the truck.

Maria leaned her head against the cool window and

closed her eyes. A light rap on the glass brought her head up with a start.

"Sorry it took so long," Joe apologized. "We're ready when you are."

"I'm ready," she replied. "You won't—"

"Go a hundred and sixty?" He chuckled, his face nearly invisible in the darkness. "I promised a sedate fifty. You can track me."

"I will," she vowed, rolling up the truck window.

Sam waved to her from the lighted interior of the expensive car, then Joe started the engine.

True to his word, Joe drove the car carefully down the highway, the old truck a dark shadow on the car's bumper.

There were no streetlights, so she couldn't see into the car, but she felt sure her son was making conversation lively for Joe.

Maria trailed them to her driveway. Sam and Joe were already out of the car by the time she'd parked the truck.

"I just want to show Joe my award," Sam said.

"No." Maria was adamant. "We had an agreement, remember? You wanted to ride in the car, but in turn you had to go straight in, take a shower and go to bed."

"Mom," he groaned.

"Another time," Joe promised. "It's getting late."

"All right." Sam glanced at his newfound friend in the halo of the porch light. "I'll see you later."

"I think my place is the next one up from here," Joe told him cheerfully. "We're neighbors. We're bound to run into each other."

Maria's heart sank. It was true. The old Hannon farm was the next place up the road, about a mile away.

However, they wouldn't be all that likely to see one another.

"I appreciate your help, Maria," Joe told her when Sam had gone inside the house.

"I did what anyone would have done. But I don't see what good it will do for you to stay here."

He laughed lightly. The sound sent a shiver up her spine, which she attributed to the late hour and the cool breeze that had picked up after the rain.

"I don't give up so easily," he told her bluntly.

"No one wants you here," she replied in as blunt a fashion. "How can you get anything accomplished like that?"

"Sometimes people have to swallow the medicine even if it doesn't taste like cherries," he replied in a cheerful tone. "I guess I'm that medicine."

Maria thought about the state of the old Hannon place but bit her tongue. She didn't have the nerve or the heart to tell him the home he was looking for wasn't to be found there.

"I guess everyone has to do what they think is best," she said, and turned to the door. "I don't envy you."

And you wish I'd go to hell and get it over with, he thought. He wondered if he'd actually consigned himself to that hot spot by staying when his every instinct was telling him to leave.

"Good night, then," she said, her voice a whisper in the darkness as the rain began to fall again.

"Good night," he told her quietly. He added, "I've seen the house, Maria."

After she'd closed the door, she thought she might have imagined the last part. How could he have seen the old house without his car? It didn't make sense. Had he walked there from town?

Probably her guilty conscience putting words in his mouth. She had been part of the scheme. Or if not actively part, then at least she didn't raise any protest.

But then she had never been one to purposely stand out or get people upset over anything.

She sighed when she saw the number of messages on her answering machine, having a good idea what those messages might be.

She stared at the little black box for a long moment, her head still pounding. Then she turned off the light without listening to the calls and slowly walked up the stairs to bed.

The rain was gone the next morning. Bright September sunlight flooded the changing leaves of the big oak trees around the farmhouse.

Maria got Sam off to school then went out to her garden. The sun was warm on her head as she worked, beginning what would probably be the last harvest of herbs for the year.

It had been a good year, a profitable year. The first since Josh's death. With any luck and a mild winter, she might be able to afford a new truck by next year.

After selling off the livestock Josh had accumulated, she had changed the old barn into a crude greenhouse that would enable her to go on raising some of her best cash crop even after the first heavy frost of fall.

Over the summer, she'd finally managed to work out a long-term deal with two of the restaurants in Rockford. They would buy whatever she could raise and deliver of fresh parsley, sage, oregano and thyme.

Being able to grow her herbs all year would ease the financial setbacks since Josh's death.

And maybe, she thought as she sat on her heels and stretched her back, she would even have enough to buy Sam a computer for his birthday next summer.

Like many couples, Maria and Josh hadn't planned for his early death or what the loss of income would mean to the ones left behind. The first year, she and Sam had barely survived while Maria had tried to patch their lives back together.

By the second year, she was fighting back and finding that she didn't have to be a victim after all. It wasn't the life she had planned, but it was the life she had, and she was going to make the best of it.

Many people, including her own family, had said that she wouldn't be able to make a go of it on her own after Josh's death. She was determined to prove them wrong.

Maria walked into the house, knowing Sam wasn't due home for another hour. She threw her dirty gloves into the washing machine then ran upstairs for a shower.

Muddy jeans and T-shirt went down the laundry chute while the water heated, making its strange gurgling and whining sounds.

It was an old house, but she and Josh had managed to get a good buy on it after they were married, when Maria had just learned she was pregnant with Sam. The house had seemed like a godsend, a way to get them out of her mother's house before the baby was born.

It was a good, sturdy house. She looked at the walls around her. It was dark, with its tiny windows, and it was cold in the winter, hot in the summer. But it was hers.

The twenty acres she owned around the house were mostly overgrown and full of rabbits. Five acres of it she'd leased to a farmer to grow alfalfa for his horses. The rest, except for the acre or so adjoining the house, wasn't used.

Josh had planned to raise cattle and horses there. It had been his dream. He had planned to buy up some land to go with what they had—the Hannon land the town had given the new sheriff.

The Hannon farm was forty acres. The land was worthwhile, but the house hadn't been lived in for over twenty years. It was falling down, rotted in most places. No running water or electricity.

When she had first learned of the plan to discourage the new sheriff and defy the county commissioners, Maria felt it was wrong, but the entire town was in on it.

Or rather, the town kept their mouths shut and let the Lightner family tell them what to do.

There was no way to present a case for fairness or to persuade them to give the new man a try. During the town meeting where it had all been decided, they had used her and Sam as living reminders that the town needed a local sheriff.

She had smiled grimly and kept her mouth shut, but she wasn't sure that had been the right thing to do. It was too late now, of course. The damage was already done. But she felt sorry for Joe Roberts. There was no way he could have known what he was walking into when they had hired him from Chicago.

She stepped out of the shower, shivering because the water heater had run out of hot water at the worst possible moment, shampoo still in her hair.

She glanced at the clock on her dresser and realized that she had taken longer than she'd expected. Sam and his friend would be home at any minute.

Quickly, she pulled on clean jeans and a white cotton button-up shirt, then brushed her hair with quick, even strokes.

She looked at her face in the mirror and saw the same face she saw every day. The blue eyes worried. The mouth getting a little more set every day.

What would Josh have wanted? she wondered. He was a fair man, but he was inclined to run with the crowd. Would he have wanted the new sheriff to be treated with less than respect? Would he have gone along with the decision to give him the old Hannon house?

Sam's call from downstairs reminded her that she didn't have time to daydream. She clipped back her shoulder-length hair and slipped her feet into tennis shoes then met her son at the top of the stairs.

"Hey, Mom!" Sam rushed toward her. "We thought you were gone."

"Hey, Mrs. Lightner!" Ronnie smiled at her then followed Sam.

"Supper's at five," she said to their backs as they disappeared into Sam's room.

Since it was Thursday, the last day of school that week, Ronnie was spending the night. That was the last bit of conversation she'd have that night. She sighed. Maybe now was the time to curl up with that book she'd meant to read for a month.

The phone rang, startling her.

It was her mother, telling her that an emergency meeting of the county commission had been called for seven that night and they wanted her to be there.

"Why?" Maria demanded. "I don't have anything to do with any of this."

"Anna Lightner seems to think your word, the wife

of the dead constable, would go a long way,'' her mother told her, pleased that her little girl's word was good for something. It had been the proudest day of her life when Maria had become a Lightner and the darkest one when they had buried Maria's young husband.

"I can't,'' Maria replied. "Sam and Ronnie are here for the night. I can't leave them alone.''

"I'll come over and stay with them,'' her mother volunteered. "Maria, this is very important. I don't think you realize that.''

"I only realize that I don't want it to have anything to do with me,'' Maria muttered tiredly. "Joe Roberts seems to be a good man. Why don't we just wait and see what happens?''

"I'll be there about six-thirty.'' Her mother ignored her remarks. "And Maria,'' she cautioned, "don't say that to anyone else.''

Maria didn't tell her that it was too late. She hung up the phone and wondered what Joe would say when he saw her.

Emergency commission meeting, she thought scornfully, getting pots and pans noisily out of the cabinet and banging them on the stove.

It was Tommy and his family trying to inflame everyone about the new sheriff. Not that anyone outside the town cared who became sheriff. Certainly the suburbs, which were growing rapidly, didn't care who was sheriff so long as he got the job done.

Not that she cared if Joe Roberts was the sheriff. In fact, she would have been happier not seeing him again. She didn't want to think about how he made her feel. She was still grieving for Josh.

At least in front of a big, noisy crowd they wouldn't

have any time alone together, she mused. He probably wouldn't even notice her with all the crowd and all the other women.

She glanced down at her clothes that had been fine for a night at home with the boys and considered changing.

Not that she wanted to look her best in case he did notice her from the crowd, she reminded herself sternly. She added a dash of bright lipstick to her pale face after she'd changed her clothes. There were butterflies in her stomach but she was just nervous about the Lightners causing trouble.

He wouldn't notice her, she repeated like a charm.

Yet a tiny voice whispered, "He might."

Chapter Three

The room in the old church was packed. Those still coming in the doors at seven would have to stand at the back. The two county commissioners who had come fretted on the dais at the front.

The other eight commissioners felt as though the matter was closed and wouldn't bother hearing the issue further. Their choice was made. Gold Springs had its first sheriff.

Some of the people of Gold Springs didn't agree.

There were quite a few unfamiliar faces in the audience. Maria guessed they were residents of the new subdivisions.

She saw Joe Roberts on the dais shaking hands with Sue Drake, one of the commissioners.

She'd probably been the one to hire him in the first place, Maria considered. How had she come to hear about him? Chicago seemed a long way away.

Maria watched Sue Drake's eyes following Joe's lean form as he moved away. Her gaze slid slowly down his back until it reached that rounded part of his anatomy clearly outlined by his uniform.

Maria glanced away, her eyes going down the dais, refusing to watch. But it only took a minute for her gaze to wander back again.

He did look very professional in his tan state trooper uniform. It hugged his broad chest and wide shoulders and made his legs look incredibly long.

He leaned over to pick up a paper he'd dropped, and Maria found herself ogling him as openly as Sue Drake had. She sucked in her breath and purposely looked away again.

"Quite a hunk," Maria's longtime friend, Amy Carlson, stated, sitting beside her in the crowded church. "I can see why you gave him a ride."

The implication—that a ride in her truck wasn't all that was involved—made Maria frown at her.

"It was all perfectly innocent."

"Of course it was." Amy sighed. "That's the part we need to talk about. It's been nearly three years, Maria. Are you going to be alone forever?"

"Why is it that everyone is worried about me being alone? No, wait," she corrected. "Everyone is worried about me not having a man."

"Because it's unnatural," Amy told her with a grin. "And because he's a damn good-looking man."

"That doesn't mean I have to sleep with him, does it?"

"Heavens, no!" Amy replied. "I think you should leave him alone so that us divorced ladies have a chance."

Maria smiled and shook her head. Amy had always been her opposite. Not afraid to voice her opinions, always the life of the party. Her bright cloud of strawberry blond hair made her easy to spot in a crowd.

They had stopped competing for men when Maria had grabbed Josh Lightner and left her friend with Tommy on a double date.

After that, Amy had married a lawyer and gone to live in Boston. She was back less than two years later, brokenhearted when she'd caught her husband with another woman.

Alone and penniless, she had managed, nonetheless, to open a small dressmaking shop that had done well almost immediately.

There had been no children. Amy had said she was grateful, but Maria doubted it. Amy was Sam's godmother and spoiled him terribly. When she saw the two of them together, Maria saw a sadness in her friend's eyes. It made her hug Sam more tightly to her.

"Looks like we're about to start the witch hunt," Amy murmured.

"Will you girls be quiet?" their former high school math teacher demanded. "You both always talked too much!"

They looked at each other then giggled, rolling their eyes. The teacher sighed and sat back in his chair, trying to ignore them.

"So, what's he like?" Amy whispered as the commissioners tried to bring the crowd to order.

"Joe?" Maria shrugged. "Just a nice guy. Sam really liked him."

"If we could get down to business?" Sue Drake glanced impatiently at her watch.

The crowd began to grow quiet. Maria spotted Tommy and his mother near the front of the church.

She was glad she didn't have to see their faces staring at her.

The old constable, Mike Matthews, stood up and looked at the crowd. His face was lined, and his eyes had faded to a pale blue. "Now, some of you still seem to have a problem with the choice of sheriff these good folks brought us."

"That's the problem right there." Tommy was on his feet, glaring at Joe Roberts. "He was their choice. Not ours."

A few people supported him, but most of the crowd remained silent.

Mike Matthews shook his head. "Tommy, I've talked with you and your family about this. The district was created between voting times. They had to appoint a sheriff. If not, we wouldn't have received the money for the new nine-one-one system. And I know we all want that."

Applause broke out randomly. People nodded and agreed.

"That's not the problem," Tommy replied. "The problem was choosing someone outside the community to take the job. You could have chosen one of us."

"We could have," Sue Drake said, "if there had been someone qualified. Setting up an entire operation from scratch takes experience. There were certain requisites for the job according to federal standards. Sheriff Roberts meets those standards."

"Maybe we should let Sheriff Roberts say a few words," remarked David Martin, the other commissioner, who nodded toward the man at the end of the line of chairs.

Joe stood, and Maria felt a hot flush hit her cheeks when his eyes locked with hers across the room. Her heart pounded, and there was a strange rolling feeling in the pit of her stomach.

She looked away first, wondering if she was about to come down with the flu. She felt strange and light-headed, breathing shallowly.

Maybe it was the crowd. The night was warm, and they were packed in like sardines. She realized suddenly that she had missed Joe Roberts's opening remarks.

"And after graduation from the academy, I worked as a policeman in Illinois for several years. I had the opportunity to join the U.S. Marshal's office, and I was there for ten years until I got the call from Commissioner Drake about the job here."

Joe looked around the crowd as he spoke.

"I believe I can set up something long-lasting here, something that will serve this area into the next millennium. One reason I accepted this job was the offer of a house and land. I plan to settle down here and become part of the community. I'd like to do my part in helping the town feel secure and watching it thrive."

Sue Drake thanked Joe warmly. "As you can see, we were fortunate to find a man as experienced as Mr. Roberts who would be willing to take the salary we could offer at this time."

"And something else to remember here." Mike Matthews joined her, presenting a united front. "In two years there will be a regular election and if Sheriff Roberts doesn't do the job you expected of him, there's plenty of time to vote in someone who will."

"But you need to give him a chance." David Martin spoke on Joe's behalf. "That's the only way we can know what he can do. His record speaks for itself, of course, and once the program is in place, federal money will be forthcoming no matter who is in office.''

"We're not satisfied with that," Tommy growled, getting to his feet. "We need someone who knows the area and the people."

"We need someone who knows how to run the kind of organization we have to create here," Mike Matthews corrected him.

"I think we should give him a chance," a tall man from the housing development spoke up, "I think he'll do a good job for the first two years."

"We think you should just sit down and shut up!" Ronnie snarled, ready to take on outsiders with a group of his peers behind him.

It looked as though the meeting would dissolve into a shouting match. Joe stood up again and claimed their attention.

"My first act as sheriff is going to be appointing deputies from Gold Springs. These people will be local homeowners who have an interest in keeping the community at its best. That would be one way for me to get to know the people and the area."

Tommy stood up and glared at him. "We just plain don't want you here!"

"I don't think you have a choice," Joe told him flatly, not taking his gaze from the angry man. "So unless you have something constructive to say, I think you should sit down and keep all the rest of this crap to yourself."

Applause broke out all over the church except, of course, from Tommy and his family and friends. Tommy turned an angry, defiant face to the crowd then walked out of the church.

"If there are any more questions, I'll be happy to answer them as best I can," Joe said.

"Whew!" Amy gasped. "That was tense!"

Maria knew Tommy wouldn't give up that easily. If he couldn't win fairly, he would find another way.

The rest of the meeting went quickly. People stood and talked for a while over coffee and cookies provided by the Daughters of the American Revolution.

"Maria!" David Martin came up to her. He kissed her cheek and hugged her close. "You've lost some weight!"

Maria glanced at the man who stood just behind him, then smiled into David's gentle blue eyes.

"Just baby fat," she countered. "How are you doing?"

"Fine. Deidre sends her love, and the boys are always after us to bring them out to play with Sam. How is he?"

"Just fine. He won second place in the science fair," she told him, acutely aware of Joe standing there, listening to them.

"I want you to meet someone," David said, bringing the new sheriff forward. "I told him that, of everyone in Gold Springs, he could depend on you. Joe Roberts, this is Maria Lightner. She's the widow of the man who was constable here for ten years. Josh and I were very good friends."

"We've met." Joe nodded and smiled slowly at her. "Nice to see you again."

"You did quite a job tonight," she told him. "Getting Tommy Lightner to shut up is nothing short of a miracle."

David laughed. "I was telling him the same thing. Is Tommy still running after you?"

Maria glanced at the floor, wishing David didn't have to tell all her secrets at once.

"You know Tommy," she said, hedging. "He doesn't know when to quit."

"I have to go." David kissed her again quickly. "Come to dinner one Sunday with Sam. Don't forget."

"I'll call Deidre," she promised.

Mike Matthews came over, nodded to Maria, then held out his hand to the new sheriff. "Anything I can do, Sheriff."

"Thanks," Joe replied, taking his hand. "I can use all of your experience, Mike."

"Don't let those Lightners rile you." He glanced at Maria cautiously. "Ma'am."

Alone in the corner of the church together, they looked away from one another and watched the crowd around them.

"People are pretty intense about the Lightners, good and bad," Joe remarked finally.

Maria nodded and smiled. "They're a hard family to ignore. You either love them or you hate them."

He regarded her intently. "David said your husband was a good man."

"He was," she replied simply, then put her empty paper cup into the trash. "I have to be going, Sheriff. I hope it works out for you."

"Thanks. Can I give you a lift for a change?"

"No, thanks. My truck is out front."

"I'd at least like to walk you out," he answered as though he'd anticipated her reply. "There's something I'd like to ask you."

"All right," she consented, curious. Her heart suddenly started pounding again, and her mouth felt dry. What could he want?

Outside the night had grown cool. There was a hint of frost in the air, although cold weather wouldn't visit them for at least a month or so.

The door closed behind them, leaving the parking lot outside the small church barely illuminated by the mercury vapor light a few doors down.

"The only time you see this many cars here," Maria remarked with a laugh, "is Founder's Day. You're famous, Sheriff."

"I think that might be infamous," he admitted, walking beside her. "It'll pass."

"Most of it," she agreed. "The Lightners won't forget."

"I'll deal with them, too," Joe said quietly.

"Well, here we are." Maria put her hand on her truck door. "It wasn't much of a walk."

"That's what I wanted to talk to you about," he said, leaning against the side of the battered pickup. "I'd like to see you. You can bring Sam, if you like. Maybe you could show me some of the sights, and I could buy you dinner."

"I don't date." She gave him the standard answer she'd used many times.

Her hands were trembling. She didn't look at him as she spoke. She was afraid that he might see that yearning that welled up in her suddenly at the idea of spending time with him. It might have been dark but her imagination made that desire feel like a hot, golden glow inside of her.

He touched her clasped hands and suddenly the nights were too long and the years ahead stared back at her. "You're shaking," he observed softly. "Scared or cold?"

"Scared," she admitted softly. Looking at Joe in the

dim light, she knew he wasn't the right one. The pain of losing Josh was too fresh, and Joe was another man cut from the same cloth. A fighter when he thought something was right. A hero.

"Don't think of it as a date then." He held her door open and deftly returned them to solid ground. "Think of it as helping a man without a kitchen."

Maria glanced at him, wondering if he could tell just by looking at her what buttons to push. He seemed to be adept at it.

And if he held her partly responsible for the mess of a place they'd given him to live, didn't she partly blame herself, as well?

"All right," she agreed carefully. "I'm making gazpacho with rosemary Tuesday night. You can come over and eat with us."

He frowned, glad that she had relented but uncertain why he had pushed them both into it. "Tuesday night."

"About seven." She started up the old truck. "You know the way."

He did know the way. He watched her drive away into the night. He could only hope that he could remember the way back.

In all his plans for his new life in Gold Springs, he hadn't planned on Maria Lightner. She was a surprise life had thrown into the equation.

At that moment, he wasn't sure if she was a good or a bad surprise. But he knew he had to find out.

By Tuesday afternoon, Joe already had a dozen more deputies than he needed for patrols. The word had spread quickly in the outlying areas. Accountants and stockbrokers were vying with lawyers and schoolteachers for the suddenly coveted positions.

None of them had ever been in law enforcement or handled a gun except in ROTC or on some far-off hunting trip. But they were the best he was likely to find. With the right training, they would do nicely. Joe promised to make his decision quickly and took the stack of applications with him.

The county was allowing him to use the old city hall, a half-ruined, tumbledown building in the middle of town. It wasn't permanent and was far from being a place to set up a sheriff's station, but it was a start.

That seemed to be all he was capable of at the time. He grimaced at his watch. Everything had become unstable, and for the first time in his life, he found himself compromising, waiting for what he wanted.

It wasn't an easy or enviable position. He slammed into his new truck and started the engine.

He was by nature a patient man, but ambition had pushed him harshly in his youth. He'd made impossible demands on himself and others. And he'd paid a heavy toll for his success.

But he had never dreamed of what he would find in Gold Springs. He pulled up the dirt driveway that was little better than a clearing in the overgrown shrubbery.

The Hannon house was collapsing, one half already fallen into decay. Birds had nested there in the spring and summer, and there was evidence of several generations of mice.

He hadn't lied when he'd told the town that the offer of a house and land had helped him decide to take the job, even though the salary had left something to be desired.

He was forty, ten years older than his father had been when he was born. He had begun to feel that time was marching on without him.

It had sounded corny to him when he'd first started to realize that something was missing from his life. But a visit to his sister's home had confirmed it. He wanted a family. Someone who'd be there at the end of the day. A place to live that wasn't a motel room.

He had moved on from every place he'd ever worked. It was the nature of the job he'd chosen. He traveled the country setting up sheriff's offices for someone else to take over. Gold Springs would be the first one that he would be setting up for himself.

The life had been his choice, but he had grown weary of it. He couldn't run forever. A house in Gold Springs was as good a place to stand his ground as any.

Well, the land was good. Half in timber, half in well-tilled farmland. It would take some work to get it in order, but he was used to working hard.

As for the house, there was only one thing to do—tear the whole thing down and start over. That was going to take more money than he had anticipated when he'd agreed to take the position.

He backed the truck toward the newly wired electric pole and turned off the engine. The little camper he'd pulled into the yard earlier would be his home for the present.

He hunched over in the tiny shower and shaved in the little sink, no bigger than a soup bowl. Using the hookup from the pole, he had electricity, and the main water line from the house gave him water. Besides a bed long enough to stretch out in, who could ask for more?

He thought about Maria while he dressed, careful not to bang his arms on the wall. Her blue eyes had started a restless anticipation in him.

He hadn't had a serious relationship in years. Usually, any relationship he had with a woman lasted only a night or two. Maria, he knew, was different.

When she looked at him, even with the tire iron in her hand, it was like electricity sizzling through him. He wanted to listen to her voice in the darkness and see her laugh in the sunshine.

Maybe he was just getting old. He even liked her kid!

But he'd seen what Josh Lightner's death had left behind for Maria and Sam. Looking into her eyes had been like looking into the past, into the fear-haunted eyes of another woman.

It had been fifteen years since his ambition and his life-style had cost him Rachel. He hadn't given himself time to slow down or to think about what had happened between them.

He looked at himself in the small mirror, stooping to see his reflection. His hair was wet, and his eyes were full of memories. Just when he thought he could leave it behind him, when he believed he'd run far enough, he came face to face with it.

There was no answer. No place he could hide. The small towns were never remote enough. And he was tired of running.

He drew a deep breath. If Gold Springs was as good a place to stand his ground as any, then dinner with Maria was as good a place to start his new life.

He drove into Maria's yard, puzzled by the five or six cars in her drive. Was something wrong?

He knocked on the door, half expecting Sam's bright eyes to greet him. Someone yelled "Come in!" and he walked into the warm kitchen.

Five pairs of eyes looked at him from the five ladies

standing around the kitchen table. They blinked in surprise, like startled owls.

"Sheriff Roberts!" one older lady called out while the others giggled like schoolgirls.

"How nice to see you!"

Everyone was introduced as they took him into the big sitting room.

"You're just in time for supper." Dennie Lambert batted her eyelashes at him.

Across the room, he caught Maria's eye as she put down a large soup tureen.

"Rosemary gazpacho?" he asked.

She nodded, only slightly uncomfortable at the look on his face. "And the Founder's Day committee for this year."

"And every year," someone laughed, and all of them giggled again.

The food was delicious and gone quickly. The five ladies devoured every word he had to say, as well as two loaves of freshly made bread. They were surprised and pleased that their new sheriff would want to take part in the Founder's Day celebration.

They asked his opinion on everything from parade permits to stopping traffic. Maria served coffee, handing him a cup as he sat in the midst of the women, fielding their questions in a quiet, polite manner.

She'd known they were coming, of course. It had seemed a way to let him know that she wouldn't see him alone. That she wasn't interested in him that way.

But watching him with the older ladies, she realized it had been a dirty trick. He had told her not to think of it as a date, but she'd known what he was expecting.

I should have told him, she thought, putting down the coffeepot after another round of refills. She shouldn't have been so worried about what he would say.

As the evening wore on and the talk continued, Maria couldn't help but notice that he didn't look her way again. He was either very angry, she decided, or he really didn't care that they weren't alone.

He listened to the women, all old enough to be his grandmother, and talked with them as though they were important to him.

That was a trait she'd noticed at once about him. He had a way of listening that made people feel as though nothing else mattered to him but what they were saying.

His dark head bent close to Tammy Marlowe's as she giggled excitedly, making Maria wonder if he wasn't giving the ladies the wrong impression. She'd thought it might be good for him to have them on his side, but she hadn't considered the idea that they might think he was flirting with them.

She began to clean away some of the mess from supper, picking up the deeper tones whenever he spoke. She felt them edge along her spine uncomfortably.

Instead of being miserable and blaming her for the evening she'd inflicted on him, Joe seemed to be having the time of his life.

She glanced his way once more, then stormed into the kitchen and stacked the dirty dishes as the sink filled with hot, soapy water.

He had the agility of a cat, she decided, plunging the dishes into the water. She began scrubbing them with a vengeful hand.

First he was willing to overlook the condition of the house they'd given him and the welcome he'd received from the town. Then, if he'd been disappointed about their date, he hadn't shown it with even the flicker of an eyelash.

"Anything I can do to help?" Joe asked, pushing his head around the corner of the door.

"Not at all," she answered, surprised that she was so angry. "Just go back in there and charm them like you did the audience at the meeting the other night."

"I'm pretty handy with a dish towel," he told her, picking one up from the sideboard.

"I don't need your help drying the dishes," she told him flatly. "I'm fine on my own."

"Are you?" he asked, pinning her with his gaze. "Is that what this is all about? Trying to show me that you don't need anyone?"

She refused to answer, furiously washing dishes until he came to stand beside her.

"Maria?"

"I'm sorry," she blurted, holding a wet plate. "I'm not good at this."

He took the plate and set it down on the cabinet with the towel he'd picked up.

"You don't have to be sorry," he assured her, not bothering to pretend that he didn't understand.

She looked at him as a tear escaped the corner of her eye. Her anguish touched a chord in him that nearly buckled his knees.

"I don't think I can handle it again." She tried to make sense. "It's been so long...."

"It's okay." He put his hand on her shoulder, hating the forlorn look in her eyes. He wanted to tell her that it wasn't a big deal, that it hadn't meant that much. But he couldn't.

She drew in a ragged breath that was his undoing as he carefully hugged her close to him. Meaning to comfort her as he would have a child, he held her against him, smelling the shampoo she used on her hair, trying not to feel the soft contours of her body against his.

Maria clung to him, receiving strength from his solid warmth until she felt his lips touch the side of her head while he murmured incoherent words of solace.

She turned her face to him. His eyes reminded her of the deep stillness of a lake, reflecting her own tears. Not daring to breathe, she stared at his mouth, a breath away from her own.

The fierceness of his kiss, a silent explosion of light and life inside her, made her close her eyes. She stopped thinking. Afterward, she would recall all the details—the clean smell of him, the warmth of his lips, the way he pressed her close to him.

She pulled away from him, shocked by the physical contact. He released her, but his gaze never left her face.

"Maria." He whispered her name, wanting to take her pain. Not wanting to lose the feeling of being whole that she'd brought to him.

With a muffled cry, she was in his arms again, hungry for that taste of him on her mouth, clinging to him as though they had always been together.

Maria felt the edge of the counter against her hip. Then he was lifting her until she was sitting on it.

Crushed against his chest, her legs straddling his sides, she opened her mouth as his kiss deepened, and a need that she hadn't known resided in her made refusal impossible.

Feverishly, she opened her eyes as his lips slipped down her neck to her breast. In a haze, she saw the five women standing a few feet away, silently watching them.

Tammy giggled, the sound alerting Joe.

"It's getting late," Dennie Lambert's sister, Mandy, remarked. "We're going now, Maria."

"Bye." Tammy giggled again.

"Good night, ladies." Joe took it in stride, turning to them. "I'm looking forward to Founder's Day."

"So are we," one of them said as the door closed behind them.

"Oh, my God," Maria whispered into the sudden quiet. She bowed her head. There would be no stopping that tidal wave from hitting the shore!

Chapter Four

There was no escaping it. The phone was ringing off the hook the next morning. Maria answered the first call, the one from her mother demanding to know what was going on, then she left the house as though the devil were on her heels.

It was cool outside, and there was a faint mist covering the ground. She sniffed appreciatively, liking the autumn perfume of earth and wood smoke from a distant neighbor's fireplace. It reminded her of the pipe blend that her father had smoked when she was a little girl.

It was strange, she thought, opening the big barn door. She could recall so many little things about her father. Yet sometimes it was hard to remember his face. He had died when she was sixteen, before she had married and Sam had entered her life. It seemed a lifetime she had lived without him.

They had been close in a way Maria had never been close with her mother. Her father wouldn't have asked what was going on with Joe. He would have sat back in his chair and waited for her to come to him.

What would he have said about the mess she had created? she wondered, pulling out the bundles of herbs she was taking into town.

She had shown Joe the back door quickly the night before. The Founder's Day committee members were still pulling out of the driveway when he was walking down the steps. No way did she want anyone to think more than that kiss had happened between them.

Even more important, she didn't want to talk to him about it. She didn't want to try to understand what it meant or why it had happened. She just wanted the whole episode to go away.

She loaded the bundles of herbs on the back of the truck, hoping the hard work would make her less edgy. She felt like biting someone's head off and she was glad that Sam was at school.

The pungent smell of lemon thyme mingled with purple basil, creating a potent cloud around her. The sun grew warmer as it rose steadily in the bright blue morning sky. Overhead, a fast-moving V of Canada geese flew by, honking as they looked for an available lake.

Maria finished wrapping a few stray bundles of oregano and sat on the tailgate, letting the wind whisper over her heated face. It was a beautiful morning. Far too nice to ruin with thoughts of the Lightners or Joe Roberts.

She finished a thermos of coffee she had been nursing through the procedure, then closed the back of the truck and tied a tarp across it.

She had done well. She congratulated herself as she

climbed into the old truck. Her father would have been proud of her.

Driving down the highway from Gold Springs, she thought about her profits, trying to work out how she might be able to swing a computer for Sam. Some of the money would have to be reinvested into next year's crop, but there would be some left over.

She could make do with her winter coat one more year, although Sam needed a new one. If she was careful with the heat and remembered to turn off the lights, she might be able to swing a computer. If not a new one, maybe a good used one.

Lost in her thoughts, it took her a minute to realize the truck wasn't making its usual clunking sound. She stepped a little harder on the gas, and the old engine spluttered and died.

Glad Sam wasn't present, she let it roll to the side of the road with a string of curses.

An hour later, after exhausting all the possibilities she knew could be wrong with the beast, she sat on the ground beside it. Her hands were filthy with grease, and there was a stain on one jeans-clad leg. She had torn her sleeve and her hair was wild.

Worse, all the while she had worked and nothing had happened, she could see the image of Sam's computer fading into a monstrous repair bill.

If she could have it repaired, she remembered, shaking her head. The last time, Billy had told her there was no point putting bad money after good into something that was just plain worn out.

But a new truck? The idea took her breath away.

"Problem, ma'am?"

It had to be Joe. Of course. Who else? She had known from the moment she discovered the truck wouldn't start that he would be driving by. The glory of the day, the bright hopes she had cherished, crumbled around her.

He was wearing his new uniform, the one everyone had so admired him in at the town meeting. He looked taller in it, more professional and less the teasing, light-hearted man she'd kissed.

"Maria?" he asked, removing his dark glasses as he squatted beside her. "Are you all right?"

"I'm fine," she replied dully. "My truck is another story."

He took in her torn, dirty appearance, stood up and held out his hand to her without hesitation.

She looked at him, liking the way his eyes stayed on hers, hating him for stirring up so much trouble in her life. She put her dirtiest hand out and let him help her to her feet.

If he noticed, he didn't comment. "I'll call for a tow truck."

"Maybe you should let me," she offered, wondering if Billy would come if the sheriff called.

"Billy and I had a little talk this morning," he informed her. "He'll come."

Maria was amazed. "I don't know what you said—"

"I told him I'd give all the towing business I came across from here to Rockford to Jack Joyner's service. He perked right up. I thought he'd been my friend for the last ten years."

Maria followed him to the back of the new sheriff's car. "Billy's always had an eye for opportunity."

He opened the trunk and handed her a clean orange rag. "Sometimes, you just have to talk sweet, ma'am."

He hadn't put on his sunglasses again, and his eyes

were intent on hers. Emotions warred silently between them, creating a long moment.

"Well." She finally broke the contact, her voice husky. She looked at her hands as she cleaned them on the rag. "I guess you should call Billy."

After the call, she sat with him in the front seat of the car waiting for the tow truck. The silence was uneasy between them.

"The county was generous," she remarked finally, looking around the interior. "Josh had to drive his own car when he went out on a call."

"It came with the job," he replied, touching the steering wheel. "How long was Josh the constable in Gold Springs?"

"About ten years," she answered, looking out the windshield at the last of the hay being harvested along the roadside.

Her heart beat a little faster, and she could feel her breath becoming more shallow as she waited for the inevitable question. How did Josh die?

"Would he have taken the sheriff's job if it had come up for him?" he wondered.

Surprised, she glanced at him. "Yes. Josh was like you."

Billy's shiny red tow truck lumbered up, yellow lights flashing, but Joe put a hand on her arm as she started to climb out of the car.

"How was he like me?"

Her gaze was direct and unflinching as a steel bullet. "He was a hero. He wanted to do what was right. Just like you."

Joe did flinch. He felt those words like tiny slivers of steel that pierced his soul. How many times had

Rachel said the same thing to him? Until finally it was too late and there were no more arguments.

Maria was nothing like Rachel, yet he saw the same fire burning in her eyes, the same anger about the way the men in their lives had chosen to live.

He watched her walk to Billy's truck, the wind blowing her hair across her face. He hadn't missed that she'd chosen to give him her greasiest hand. She was mad about last night.

He wasn't sure why she was mad or if she was mad at him or herself. He didn't think she knew, either.

The more he knew about Maria Lightner, the more he wanted to know. She was strong in a way that made him want to help her.

You would always know where you stood with her. He grimaced as he got out of the car. Once she'd made up her mind.

"I told you last time, Maria," Billy was saying as he hooked the tow bar to the truck.

"Maybe it's not so bad," she replied hopefully.

Billy climbed to the back of the truck and turned on the electric crank. "Not so bad? Maria, if this thing was a horse, you would have shot it a year ago out of kindness."

"Will you look at it anyway?"

"I'll look at it," he replied with a heavy sigh, telling her plainly that looking at it wouldn't do much good.

"If everything's in hand—" Joe began, glancing at his watch.

"We got it covered here, Sheriff," Billy said with a big grin. "I'll take Maria and the truck back to town."

Joe nodded, replacing his dark glasses. "Thanks. I'll see you both later."

Maria watched the brown and gray squad car drive

away, thinking that Joe was in a hurry to get rid of her. She was glad, of course. The less time she spent in his company, the better. She didn't want to notice his hands or the way he spoke or the shape of his ears.

She didn't want to think of him as anything except the new sheriff. She wished him well, but she didn't want him to be an important part of her life.

She particularly never wanted him to kiss her again. She never wanted that mind-numbing, stomach-crunching, toe-curling experience again.

Billy complained all the way to the garage. The sheriff had threatened his livelihood unless he worked with him. What else could he do?

Maria told him she understood.

"I don't think Tommy will," he retorted as he turned the truck in at the garage. "He said he's through with trying to scare the sheriff out of town. He's going to get up a petition to have him removed from office."

"I don't think that's going to happen," Maria told him with a quick shake of her head. "He might as well wait and run against him for sheriff in two years."

Billy nodded. "That's just what I told him. His daddy told him the same thing, but you know Anna Lightner. She's not satisfied with the way things are."

Maria did know what Mrs. Lightner was like. The first time Josh had brought her home for Sunday dinner, his mother had looked down her nose at Maria as though she was a strange insect.

"So this is the girl?" she'd asked, making Maria want to climb under a chair.

Josh had put an arm around both of them. "I'm going to marry Maria, Mom."

Mrs. Lightner had made it clear what she'd thought about that idea. Yet Josh had teased her and kissed her powdered cheek, and they'd had dinner as a family. Josh was the only one of her three sons who could get around their mother that way. She hadn't given her blessing on their marriage but she hadn't done anything to stand in their way, either.

Billy whistled loudly, and Maria blinked, bringing herself to the present.

"This is worse than I thought," he told her finally.

Maria's heart sank. "But can you fix it?"

"Maria, it would cost more than this pile of scrap metal is worth. You need a new truck."

She glanced at her watch. There was no point in worrying about the truck. She had her deliveries to make, or everything she'd worked for would be lost.

She called around, trying to find someone with an available truck she could borrow, but friends and family were either busy or out of town. It crossed her mind that people were deliberately giving her the cold shoulder. After all, she had helped the sheriff. Tommy had warned her.

But that was silly. She shook her head and pushed herself to think. She had to know someone with a truck who could give her a lift into Rockford. There had to be a way.

"Sheriff!" She heard Billy hail Joe as he entered the garage.

Maria did a double take. Hadn't Joe been driving a pickup when he'd left her house last night?

She pushed that thought out as quickly as it weaseled its way into her brain. She wouldn't, she couldn't ask him for his help.

Even though, a sly voice reminded her, she had helped him with his car.

No, she thought, the phone still in her hand.

"I thought I'd check here on my way home and see if you needed a lift," Joe offered lightly.

"Well," she began as the battle raged inside her, "I could use a lift—"

"I'd be glad to take you—"

"Into Rockford," she finished before she lost her nerve. She told him the herbs were in her truck and that they needed to go into town or she would lose her contracts for next spring.

"I'm off duty in ten minutes," he replied simply. "We'll get the truck and come back."

She stared at him, feeling the wall she'd tried to build against him begin to soften at the edges. "That's it? I mean, you'll do it?"

He nodded, a smile playing around his lips like a shadow. "You'll have to buy me lunch."

"No problem," she agreed with a deep breath of relief. "Thanks."

"My pleasure, ma'am." He tipped his hat and allowed his eyes to roam across her appreciatively.

Maria smiled, too, glad that she'd taken a moment to clean up and smooth her hair. A clean sweater hid the torn and dirty place on her shirt.

Not that it mattered, she reminded herself sternly.

An hour later, she was sitting on the front seat beside him as the truck ate up the miles between Gold Springs and Rockford. It had been exasperating loading the herb bundles into the back of Joe's truck. A few of the bundles had been broken, but most were still intact.

Maria had driven with him to pick up his truck. She had waited outside the small camping trailer while he'd changed his clothes.

"There's two rooms, if you want to wait inside," he'd told her politely.

But she preferred to wait in the sunshine. He left the outside door open and disappeared into the tiny back bedroom. She couldn't resist glancing inside the self-contained home on wheels.

There was a doll-size table with one chair and a small refrigerator and stove. The bathroom was barely a closet with a hand-held shower and a drain. She looked at the drainage platform and wasn't sure she could fit on it. How did he manage?

It made her feel guilty all over again since she'd been part of the decision to let the new sheriff have the Hannon place. Maybe she didn't actively dream up the idea, but she didn't argue with anyone about it, either. The man had come to Gold Springs to do a job and expecting a decent place to live, and instead, he was living in a tiny shell of a place. They should all feel ashamed.

As she waited for him, she looked around for the personal things that separate one home from another. She saw his shooting trophies, his law enforcement degree and his bachelor's degree from college.

His razor and comb were teetering on the edge of a tiny sink. She stepped inside to move them into a less precarious position. There was a picture of a woman and three children that she guessed was probably his sister. Beside it was a college ring with a blue stone and his name on it. Next to that was a small pistol with a silver filigree handle.

The man traveled light, she thought, putting the ring down quickly when she heard him opening the door of the next room.

She took a quick step outside the trailer. Where, she wondered, was he sleeping? The room she'd glimpsed didn't look big enough for a bed.

"Sorry," he said, smoothing his hair with an impatient hand. "Maneuvering in there takes some getting used to."

She nodded, glad she wasn't caught snooping. "That's okay. I appreciate the help."

She realized she didn't know much about Joe Roberts. He seemed to be a loner, a man who didn't settle in one place for very long.

"No problem." He gave her a sidelong glance. It was easy to remember the first time he'd seen her with the tire iron in her hands. She didn't look any more comfortable than he felt being alone with her.

"Where's Sam today?" he wondered, making conversation after a few silent miles in the truck.

"He's at school," she murmured, thinking about her truck.

"I can pick him up if he needs a ride," he volunteered, "unless Billy is going to have your truck fixed."

She sighed. Heavily. "He's not going to have it fixed. He says it's dead this time. I guess I'll have to replace it."

Joe hated to mention that he guessed she was short on cash. It wasn't hard. From the things Sam had told him and the fact that she was driving the old truck, it was a closed case.

He glanced out the side window at the remaining leaves swept by the strong wind along the roadside. "That's too bad. If there's anything I can do—"

She shook her head and laughed ruefully.

"Something funny?"

"I guess I'm trying to understand you. How can you offer to help any of us?"

"It's not hard to understand," he replied, sparing her

a glance. "Gold Springs is my new home. I plan to do whatever I can for the community. Protect and serve."

Nothing personal, she noticed, relieved and annoyed.

"Even after we deceived you? After seeing the Hannon place—"

"It's good land," he told her. "The house leaves something to be desired, but that'll come."

"You are an incredibly patient and forgiving man," she remarked. "I would have driven off in my Porsche and consigned us all to the devil."

He smiled. "I've done that before. The world runs in circles, Maria. We keep coming back to the things we don't finish."

Maria stared out the window, not knowing what to say. Joe Roberts was too good for Gold Springs.

"I thought you might be able to help me out." He changed the subject after she had been quiet for a few moments. "I'm looking for someone to work part-time helping me get the sheriff's office set up. Sort of a secretary, switchboard operator and consultant rolled into one. I need someone familiar with emergency calls who can learn the system and teach it to other people."

Maria looked at her chapped hands, noticing that she had a broken fingernail from her morning's efforts. He was offering her a job. He knew they were tight on money and he was giving her a chance to work something out. She knew it as clearly as if he'd come right out and asked her.

She was touched, but at the same time, she was wary. It might be better, if they needed extra money, for her to go to work at the pizza restaurant in Rockford.

"I'll tell anyone I think might be interested," she replied carefully, smiling at him, admiring the way the sunlight touched the soft blue of his flannel shirt. "You should probably put an ad in the paper."

He stopped the truck at the first red light at the edge of Rockford. "I could do that," he agreed, adding silently, *And I should do that. But I want you.*

She directed him to the health food store that was her first stop.

"I can handle this," she told Joe when he got out of the pickup.

He nodded. "I can help."

"I'm just going to pick up a few bundles and take them inside," she argued.

He opened the back door. "You take care of the business part and let me do the hauling." She protested. He said, "Nothing personal, but lunch comes faster this way. Right?"

Maria agreed then stood at the back door with the owner while Joe brought in several bundles of herbs.

"Hired help?" the woman asked, never taking her eyes from Joe's long legs while he laid the bundles on the floor near the pantry.

"My brother," Maria quipped. "He's married. Ten kids."

"Ten?" The woman was both impressed and disillusioned. She looked at Joe with a wary reverence when she shook his hand as they left the store.

"What's with her?" he asked as he brushed herbs from his shirt.

"She doesn't like men," Maria answered, climbing into the truck.

"Oh," he replied casually. "Where now?"

They hit the second stop, and the chef at the Orchid Family Restaurant shook their hands heartily, promising to buy herbs from Maria again in the spring.

Maria dropped off the last of the herbs at the farmer's market then, checks in hand, she asked Joe to head for the bank.

"My first real profit," she told him proudly, forgetting for a minute the distance that she'd wanted to keep between them.

It felt natural, at that high moment of triumph, to throw her arms around his neck and hug him quickly.

He took one look at her shining eyes and flushed cheeks and it seemed just as natural for him to lower his mouth those few inches to rest lightly on hers.

She stepped back when his arms would have gone around her. "Thanks. For your help, I mean."

He frowned as the moment passed. "Just returning the favor."

He waited in the truck while she went into the bank, brooding over the hasty flashes of heat between them.

What did he want? They'd only known each other a few days. And if he wasn't careful, he would scare her away from the job at the sheriff's office. He needed her experience there as much as she needed the job.

What he didn't need was that ache of vulnerability when he looked at her. They had both lost. Seeing her grief made him face his in a way he hadn't for years. If he had ever really faced it.

Maria returned.

"Lunch?" she asked, a generous smile on her face.

He looked at her, captivated by the curve of her lips, and his words of warning faded into the sunlight that haloed her head. "I'm starved."

"Good. I know a nice place down by the lake."

He drove through town at her direction, promising himself that he would eat lunch with her without rushing his fences. He wouldn't push her and he wouldn't touch her.

They sat on a wrought iron bench in the sunlight and ate burritos from a street vendor, the leaves cascading from the trees above them. Twice, they had to fish russet colored oak leaves from a glass of soda, but the last of the warm weather made it worthwhile.

Conversation was general. The weather would turn cool soon. The holidays were coming already. The year was nearly over.

"I couldn't believe it when I saw Christmas trees being advertised, and it's not even October!" She laughed and threw the last piece of her burrito shell to a few waiting ducks.

"I spent last Christmas on the road," he told her quietly, looking out over the lake that reflected the blue of the clear sky above it.

"But your sister—I mean, you have family." She hesitated.

"I was trying to get to her house," he explained. "It took an extra day because of the bad weather." He looked at her. "I did deliver a baby on the way."

Maria's eyes widened. "Really? How?"

"The mother was trapped in an accident. The snowplow was on the way with the ambulance and the highway patrol but I was the first person on the scene."

"Were they all right?"

"They were both fine," he replied. "A few minutes later, everybody else got there and I went on. That's when I decided to take this job."

"Why?" she asked, holding his eyes.

"Because it seemed to me that I was always going on to somewhere else." He drew a deep breath and smiled at her slowly. "I wanted a home. I wanted to be somewhere to see some of those babies grow up."

Maria looked away from his earnest face and finished her soda silently, then tossed the cup into the trash barrel. "Josh helped deliver a string of babies while he was constable. It was one of his favorite calls."

Joe tossed away his cup, watching her for a long moment while she walked to the lake. He had promised himself he wouldn't pry, but it seemed he had no choice. Guilt, remorse and a powerful sense of responsibility won out over common sense.

"Tell me about Josh, Maria," he invited when he reached her side.

In silent agreement, they started to walk along the path that circled the lake. The dozen or so ducks quacked and waddled after them, hoping for more food.

"Josh," she mused, not looking at her companion. "He always tried to do the right thing. He was as opposite from Tommy as it's possible for two brothers to be. He was funny and he could charm the birds from the trees."

"And you loved him," he finished, a painful knot forming in his chest. He was jealous of a dead man. A dead man who could have been him. Who would never see his son grow up.

"And I loved him." She looked at him, sweeping her hair from her face with a careless hand. "We were married ten years, straight out of high school. I never dated anyone seriously before I met him, and I haven't dated anyone since he…since he died."

He could hear the slight quiver in her voice and wished he could change the subject, but he had to know. "What happened to him, Maria?"

She sighed and wished she didn't have to tell it. She realized she had never said it out loud. Everyone had known what happened. "He went out one evening after dinner. Frank Martin's wife called and said that he was beating her again."

Maria glanced at Joe and tried to smile. "They had ten kids together but they couldn't keep from hurting each other. Mike Matthews used to tell us stories about Frank's mother and father...they were the same way."

They walked on for a few minutes with only the sound of traffic from the road and the laughter of a few small children playing in the park.

"Anyway, this time, he had a gun. They said he was crazy with it, firing in the air and threatening to kill them all. The highway patrol had come out from Rockford, but because Josh had seen Frank through it so many times, they let him try to handle the situation."

Maria paused and looked over the sparkling lake. "Josh could talk anybody into anything. They all heard the gunfire after he went into the house. Then he came out with the gun in his hand and collapsed at their feet. Frank had fired—randomly, they said, but he had hit Josh. He died on the way to the hospital."

Chapter Five

"Saying I'm sorry seems out of place," he said finally, as they stood staring at the lake.

She shivered and started to walk again. Cold despite the warm sun, she wrapped her arms across her chest. "Afterward, Frank was convicted of murder. His wife and kids moved close to the prison so they could be near him."

"And Tommy took Josh's job as constable?"

"No," she answered, shaking her head. "The talk had already started about finding a full-time sheriff to take his place. Mike Matthews took his old job back. Tommy stayed on as his deputy, thinking he'd get the job when the time came."

"So Josh died a hero?" Joe asked quietly.

"A hero," she repeated. "They gave him a twenty-one-gun salute and gave me a flag and his badge."

Joe nodded. "He was a good man."

Maria stopped walking and faced him angrily. "Don't you see? He was a good man and a hero to a lot of people. But he's dead because of needing to do the right thing. If he had stayed home and raised cattle the way he'd always dreamed, he would still be alive."

Joe understood what she was saying but disagreed. "He wanted to make a difference." Hadn't that always been his answer to Rachel?

"He did, a big difference in our son's life and my life. His mother goes to put fresh flowers on his grave every week. That was the difference he should have been making. Frank and his wife still love each other and plan on being together when he gets out of prison. How much of a difference did he make to their lives?"

She walked toward the truck and Joe followed, knowing there wasn't anything he could say that would make a difference. He watched her quickly wipe a gleaming tear from the side of her face and bitterly regretted that he had broached the subject.

What was he doing? Once again trying stubbornly to defend a life-style that had killed Rachel and taken Maria's husband. Hadn't that been why he'd decided not to have a family?

Maria took deep breaths to calm herself. The pain should have been dulled, but it was just as fresh as the night they'd come to tell her that Josh was dead. She was embarrassed by her outburst and wanted to apologize to Joe but couldn't find the words.

He'd asked about Josh. Now he knew.

It was easier for her to understand why she couldn't be involved with the man sitting beside her on the way home.

Reliving those feelings had brought them all back. The pain of Josh's loss and the feeling of betrayal that he was gone reminded her that Joe Roberts was cut from the same cloth. There was every chance that he would end up the same way.

Maria didn't want to be the one left grieving this time. She wouldn't put Sam through anything so painful again.

Yet, when she dared a quick glance at him as she got into the truck, she was sorry she had raged at him.

"I'm sorry," she said across the steady hum of the tires. "I didn't mean to sound like it was your fault."

He shrugged. "I asked. I'm sorry I caused you so much pain telling it again."

"That's the funny part," she replied, smiling. "I've never told anyone. Everyone knew when Josh died and how he died. Even Sam's teacher had told him by the time I went and picked him up from school. You're the first person I've told."

"It might be a good thing," he remarked softly, wanting to touch the hand on the seat between them. He refrained with a large margin of will. "Maybe telling somebody about it will help you start to work through it."

"I've been working through it," she answered tartly, looking away from him.

Joe took one look at her profile and knew he should shut his mouth, but he knew about running away from the truth. "It's not wrong to grieve for someone you loved, but that bitterness is going to eat away at you."

"I think I have a right to feel bitter," she returned swiftly. "Josh was killed for no good reason."

"He was doing what he thought was right," Joe reminded her. "He was doing what he wanted to do with his life. What more can any of us ask out of life?"

She was astonished. No one had said anything of that kind to her before. "Sam and I have had to fight just to keep clothes on our backs and a roof over our heads. Sam has had to live without a father and I have had to live without the man I loved because of a principle!''

At a stop light, Joe turned and faced her across the width of the seat, his dark eyes vivid in his lean face. ''He was the man you loved because of those things. Don't you get it? He would have been Tommy or someone else if he hadn't lived his life that way. What we are defines what we do. Either you were in love with Josh or you were in love with the man you thought Josh should be. Which was it?''

Maria felt as though he had dealt her a body blow. She had never meant to discuss the subject with him or with anyone. What she felt, her loss of Josh and the life they'd planned, was too personal. She hugged it to her as she did her love for her son and refused to allow a stranger to question it.

She didn't answer his question, didn't speak again until they had reached the turn into Gold Springs.

''Sam's at his friend's house by now. If you'd take me to get him,'' she promised frostily, ''I won't bother you again.''

He sighed. ''Where?''

She pointed out the way down the steep gravel road to a large farmhouse that needed a fresh coat of paint.

''I can get a ride from here, thanks,'' she said quickly, hopping out of the truck before he had time to turn off the engine.

''I can take you both home,'' he offered, knowing she wouldn't accept. Her eyes were cold enough to freeze his soul from across the cab.

''Thanks, anyway. Goodbye, Sheriff.''

''Think about the job, Maria,'' he said as she started

to walk away. "You have better qualifications for it than anyone else in Gold Springs."

She stopped and stared at him. "Don't forget that ad in the paper, Sheriff. You're bound to find someone who wants to work for you."

He wanted to hit his head on the steering wheel as he paused before pulling down the long driveway.

The similarities between Joe and Josh Lightner must have ended with them both being law enforcement officers. Josh could charm the birds out of the trees. He, on the other hand, had no such talent.

It was for the best, he decided.

Maria was the ghost of regret that Rachel had always argued she would be if something happened to him. It was like watching a bad mirror image of his own past. He didn't need those memories and that grief at a moment he was fighting for his survival and a new start.

Plans surged ahead in the following week for the Founder's Day celebrations. Girl Scout Troop 119 worked on a float depicting the gold strike that brought settlers to Gold Springs. Prizewinning cake recipes were taken out of files and tested.

Sheriff Roberts and his deputies had their hands full with several drunk drivers and a few domestic violence cases. The county had sent another squad car, and nightly patrols of the new housing developments had brought good wishes from their inhabitants. Everyone felt safer seeing the cars following their nightly routes.

The Lightner family seethed and kept their distance. Tommy circulated a petition to have the county recall the new sheriff, but only a handful of his friends signed the paper. The effort died quietly.

Maria and Sam had dinner Sunday afternoon in the

Lightners' elegant home. Sam was their only grand-child, and despite Anna Lightner's ambivalence toward Sam's mother, she doted on the child.

"How are things going, Maria?" Joel Lightner asked while his wife scurried into the kitchen to find some of Sam's favorite ice cream.

"Pretty good," she answered, sitting back in her chair. She was at ease since Tommy and the youngest Lightner son, Ricky, had left before the meal had started. "The harvest was good this year. I think next year will be even better."

"I heard about your truck," Joel said, trying to offer his help in as delicate a manner as possible. His pale eyes fastened on his daughter-in-law. He knew Maria could be headstrong and too proud for her own good.

"I'm going to buy another one from Billy. He's will-ing to let me make payments on one he worked on last month," she assured him. "We'll be okay."

"I'm sure." He smiled kindly down the length of white linen tablecloth at her. "But you know if we can help—"

"I know," she said, grateful. "We'll be okay, Joel."

"Your sheriff friend has made a mess of things just like we were all afraid he would," Anna Lightner said as she returned from the kitchen.

"Oh, Anna." Her husband tried to stall the tirade but was silenced with an iron stare.

"He doesn't know when to step in and where to mind his own business," she continued as though Joel hadn't spoken.

Maria watched her son eat his ice cream. "He does his job, I think, Anna. Most people seem to like him."

"The boys have had races out at Downs Crossroads for years now—since I was in school. It has never concerned anyone before," she told Maria. "He gave some of the boys a hard time last weekend."

Maria shrugged, crossing her arms defensively. "I think racing is illegal. Maybe that's why he thought it was his business."

"Tommy and Josh raced out there," Anna Lightner reminded her. "Are you saying they did something illegal?"

"No." Maria backed down, not wanting to argue with the woman. "I'm saying that Joe Roberts does what he thinks is right. Just like Josh did. Are you saying that was wrong?"

If looks could kill... Maria shivered under Anna Lightner's belligerent stare.

"I'm saying that this town doesn't take well to outsiders coming along and trying to meddle. Your friend the sheriff would do well to leave things alone or he might find himself doing some explaining about his own life."

Maria started to tell her he wasn't "her friend the sheriff," but she held her tongue. Had Anna managed to dig up some dirt to hold over the sheriff's head?

They left about two o'clock. Tommy came home just in time to offer to take Maria home. The elder Lightner was glad of the chance to hide in his study and waved to his daughter-in-law without a second thought as she climbed into the car with Tommy at the wheel.

Maria had her reservations but she held them back, knowing Tommy wouldn't try anything while Sam was with her.

"I've been thinking about getting you a horse for Christmas this year." Tommy beguiled Sam with a smile that was reminiscent of his father. "What would you think of that?"

"A horse? Wow! That would be great, Uncle Tommy!"

"Would you rather have a big black like Dancer or would you rather have a nice pony?" Tommy laid his foot heavily on the gas pedal and left the driveway with a shower of gravel.

"A big black like Dancer," Sam answered quickly. "Could I really have a horse?"

"No," Maria told him. "Uncle Tommy shouldn't promise you things that we can't afford to feed."

Tommy groaned. "Maria, you're getting to be a spoilsport. I'll feed the horse for you, honey. I wouldn't create a burden for you and Sam."

"Would you please slow down?" she asked as he raced up the side road to the main street. "We aren't in any hurry."

"Can I have a horse if Uncle Tommy feeds him?" Sam asked.

"No," Maria answered, glaring at Tommy.

Sam turned to look at her and frowned. "There's a police car behind us. Do you think it's Joe?"

Maria looked through the back windshield and put a hand to her head. The blue lights on the new patrol car were flashing, and the siren turned on and off once, signaling them to pull over.

Tommy pulled the car to the side of the road, glaring in the rearview mirror at Maria as though it was her fault.

"License and registration, please," the new deputy insisted. It wasn't Joe.

Maria recognized one of the men from the town meeting who had signed up to help the sheriff. He lived in a new housing community.

"What's the problem, Deputy?" Tommy inquired lazily.

"You were speeding, sir. Could I see your license and registration, please?"

Tommy angrily produced his license and the car registration. "I wasn't speeding."

The deputy looked at his license closely. "You obviously didn't realize how fast you were going, Mr. Lightner."

"This road isn't posted," Tommy argued. "That means you can go any speed on it."

"From your house to this intersection, there are two posted speed signs of forty-five, Mr. Lightner. I clocked you doing well over sixty."

"I think you better get a new clock then, Deputy," Tommy told him with a laugh, looking at Maria and Sam to see if they caught the joke.

The deputy made up his mind. "If you'll step to my car, uh, the patrol car, Mr. Lightner—"

"You aren't giving me a ticket?" Tommy demanded in disbelief.

"I'm only going to issue you a warning on the speeding, sir, but I have to issue you a ticket for not wearing your seat belt. It's state law. If you'll step back to the car—"

"You can't—"

"Don't make this any worse, sir," the deputy warned sternly. "Right now, we're only talking a seat belt violation."

Tommy grunted, but he accompanied the deputy to the patrol car.

"Is he going to arrest Uncle Tommy?" Sam wondered as they waited.

"No," Maria countered. "He's just going to give

Uncle Tommy a ticket. That's what happens when you break the law, Sam.''

"You'd think Uncle Tommy would know better,'' Sam told her. "He wanted to be the sheriff.''

"Everybody makes mistakes,'' Maria answered quietly. She saw Tommy stalking to the car. "Hush now.''

Tommy slammed the door closed, didn't put on his seat belt and spun gravel behind him as he raced to the main road.

"We'll see about this,'' he promised, running his hand through his spiky hair. He looked in his rearview mirror at the police car.

"Tommy, take us home,'' Maria insisted, afraid for Sam and herself.

"After we go have a word with your boyfriend. He better call off his deputies and rip up this piece of paper, if he knows what's good for him. We've got his number now.''

Sam dared a questioning look at his mother. Maria shook her head. It was the same veiled threat Anna had proposed at the house. What had they managed to find out about Joe?

Tommy turned sharply off the main road onto the overgrown driveway that marked the Hannon place. He scanned the property for its owner. "Stay here,'' he advised Maria. "I'll be back when I'm finished with this.''

Maria waited until he'd slammed the door and started to walk away. "Get out, Sam. We aren't going to ride home with Uncle Tommy, after all.''

"I told you to stay in the car, Maria,'' Tommy yelled, turning back.

"I'm not getting in the car again with you,'' she said

firmly. "You're acting like a maniac, Tommy. You've let all of this drive you crazy."

"Maria—" he threatened.

"Maria?" Joe came around the corner of the old house, surveying the situation through narrowed eyes. "Is there a problem?"

"I'll tell you what the problem is." Tommy stalked toward him. He threw the violation ticket on the ground at the sheriff's feet. "One of your boys gave me this ticket."

Joe glanced at the paper on the ground. "Maybe you'd better pick it up then, Tommy. That's a legal document."

"This is what I think of your legal document." Tommy spit the words out and ground the paper under his booted foot. "And you. I had a little talk with some of your friends from Chicago. You'd better watch your step, Sheriff. Come on, Maria."

"No, Tommy. We'll walk," she told him bluntly.

"Fine." He paused for an instant, looking at Sam's frightened face. He seemed to relent. "Come on, Maria. I'm okay."

"We'll walk, Tommy," she repeated intently. "Go home."

"I will," he answered with a glare at the sheriff. "Don't forget what I said, Sheriff! This is just starting between us."

The rear tires of the new Cadillac spun as he backed down the driveway.

Sam clutched his mother's hand, and Maria knelt beside him in the wet leaves, hugging him to her.

"It's okay," she assured him, kissing his forehead. "Uncle Tommy's just angry."

"Real angry," Sam agreed, sniffling. "I wasn't scared."

She shook her head. "I didn't think so. Uncle Tommy wouldn't hurt you, Sam."

"I know," he lied in a small voice.

Joe took a deep breath and stopped himself from following Tommy down the road. There was no point in pushing him. If something was going to happen between them, he wanted the law to be on his side.

He joined Maria and Sam. "I haven't seen you in a few days, Sam. What have you been up to?"

"Hi, Joe." The boy looked at him. "Should I call you sheriff now?"

"I think you can call me Joe since you knew me before I was officially the sheriff," Joe told him with a smile. "There's something over here I'd like you to have a look at."

"What?" Sam was up at once, ready to go. "What are you doing out here?"

"I'm tearing the old house down but I'm saving what I can find that's still good," Joe explained with a quick glance at Maria, who smiled self-consciously.

She followed them behind the mostly rotted structure, seeing the work he'd already done. He'd pulled down and saved the boards that could be used again.

Joe led them to the back right corner of the house. "Look what I found." A set of double doors opened into the ground.

"A root cellar," Maria exclaimed. "Our house had one when I was a little girl. People stored their potatoes and canned goods in places like these."

"What's down there?" Sam asked Joe.

"I was just about to find out," Joe replied. "Want to come?"

"You bet!" Sam grinned, helping him open the doors.

There was a heavy, pungent odor of earth and something rotten in the old cellar. It was black as they descended the slippery stairs but Joe flicked on a flashlight.

"Careful," he advised Maria, looking at her strappy sandals.

"I'm not exactly dressed for adventuring," she admitted with a wry smile at her pale blue skirt and blouse.

"No," he agreed, "but we can overlook that, can't we, Sam?"

"Oh, sure," Sam said generously. "We were at Grandma's. Mom always dresses up when we go there. She looks good, doesn't she, Joe?"

Sam stood between the two adults in the cramped root cellar and smiled, waiting for an answer.

"She looks great." Joe looked from her sandals to her face in the half light from the flashlight. "But she always looks great."

"Not in the morning," Sam told him with a laugh and a roll of his eyes. "She gets up like a zombie."

"Sam!" Maria stopped his personal remarks. "Are we down here to explore the root cellar or what?"

Sam smiled at Joe, who shrugged, and they started to look along the walls.

"There's probably not much here," Maria said, leaning down to touch the cool earth wall. "The Hannons weren't well off. They were just an old couple who raised their kids and worked the land until they died."

"What happened to them?" Joe wondered, using the flashlight to peer at mostly empty shelves.

Maria searched her memory. "I think Mrs. Hannon had an accident, fell down in the yard or something. She was out in the cold for a while and developed pneumonia. Mr. Hannon never recovered after she died. He just wasted away."

Silently, they looked in the dark corners of the root cellar and found a few random objects. A rusted pot and a copper duck covered with bright green oxidation sat beside each other on a shelf. There were some bits of blue glass, and some green bottles and a few rotted potato sacks.

Sam called out when he found something shiny on the floor. "It's money," he exclaimed.

Joe turned the light on it and brushed it with his fingers. "I think it's a silver dollar."

"Really? A silver dollar?"

"Probably an old one," Joe elaborated. "Let's take it outside."

It was good to be out of the cellar in the bright, warm sunshine. Maria watched as Joe and Sam, their heads bent close together, cleaned the coin and examined it carefully.

She knew Sam liked Joe. Of course she'd be lying if she said she didn't like him. That wasn't the point. She didn't want to wake up one morning and find out she more than liked him.

But there wasn't anything she could do about her son. She knew Sam wanted a father, and he probably thought Joe Roberts fit the bill.

"It is a dollar," Sam yelped as Joe confirmed it. "It's an 1890 silver dollar, Mom."

Maria looked at it shining in the yellow sunlight after years in the darkness. The elaborate Liberty on the coin stared at her.

"It's beautiful," she murmured. "Probably worth some money, too."

"You'll have to find out," Joe told him.

"You mean I can keep it?" Sam asked in wonder.

"Sure," Joe answered easily. "You found it. It wouldn't have been much of a treasure hunt if you couldn't keep the treasure."

"Thanks, Joe!"

"I think I have a pouch you can keep that in." The sheriff considered. "Climb in the camper and look in the first drawer on the left."

"You're going to pull the whole house down?" Maria asked when Sam had run toward the camper.

"I'm going to salvage what I can," he explained. "Then I'm going to rebuild. It's a good place for a house. Look at those pecan trees!"

She did look at the towering trees, their fruit covering the ground at her feet.

"You're good with Sam," she told him, squinting at him in the bright sunlight. "You should have your own family."

He shook his head. "My life's not good for a family." *You should know,* he added silently.

"I'm sorry about the other day," she ventured, turning away from him. "I know I'm too sensitive about Josh and everything that happened."

"I'm the one who's sorry." He caught her eye as he caught her hand. "I didn't have any business pointing out your problems for you. You were right to bite my head off."

"Did I?" she asked, letting a smile play on her lips. His hold on her hand was light. There was nothing intimidating about his touch. She felt comfortable with him at that moment.

He wondered at that hint of a smile, but was happy to see it. "I wandered around for hours without it."

Maria laughed. "I promise not to do it again. I think you're going to need your head."

"No one seemed to notice when it wasn't there," he told her quickly. "It might just be ornamentation."

"I found it," Sam yelled, running from the camper. He held out a small black velvet pouch with a drawstring.

Joe took it from him and held it open while Sam dropped the coin into it. "Keep it another hundred years and it really will be worth something."

Sam's blue eyes were shining. "Wait till I show everybody."

"We should be going," Maria told him. "Joe has a lot to do, and you still have homework."

"Let me give you a ride," Joe offered.

Maria waved her hand. "We can walk. It's not that far. Thanks, anyway."

"I'll be glad when Billy has the new truck ready," Sam told him confidingly.

"When is that?" Joe looked at Maria, but it was Sam who answered.

"Tomorrow. I had to give up my computer this year for it, but that's okay."

Joe hated to look up at Maria from her son's matter-of-fact face, but he had no choice. She was embarrassed, of course.

"It's okay," he assured her with a smile.

"Thanks," she muttered, urging her son toward the driveway. "Good luck with the house."

"Good luck with the truck," he returned, stopping himself from offering the job at the office again. If she decided she was interested, she'd let him know. In the meantime, they'd called a truce of sorts, anyway. Talking was always a step in the right direction.

"You don't have to tell Joe everything that happens to us," Maria explained to Sam as they walked down the gravel road. Tall yellow grasses swayed in the wind, and she pulled the clip from her hair.

"Joe's a good guy, like Dad," Sam told her. "He doesn't mind knowing that stuff."

"He might not mind, but I do," she answered. "Our personal life isn't something to share with him, even if he is a good guy."

"Okay," Sam agreed finally. "Can we have pizza for supper?"

Maria looked to the heavens for help but knew there wouldn't be any forthcoming for another ten years. When Sam was an adult, he would understand. Before then, he was an open, generous little boy. He didn't mind knowing other people's problems, and he wanted to share his own.

"Thanks for telling him that it was okay about the computer, anyway." She touched his shoulder. "I'm glad you understand."

He looked at her and smiled. "You should get married again, Mom. I won't be a kid forever, you know."

"I know." She tickled his ribs as they ran the last few yards to their house. "And I'm glad! Someday you'll be a little boy's father, and I can remind you about all the things you did."

Sam laughed and dodged away from her. "Not me! I'm not going to marry some yucky girl."

"Oh, but you want me to marry some yucky guy, huh?"

"Guys aren't yucky," Sam replied fiercely. "At least, Joe isn't."

Maria pushed her key into the door lock and ran into the house before Sam could jump up on the side of the porch.

"It's cold." He joined her in the kitchen as she turned on the light.

Maria sighed, seeing the last of her options disappear. "Sam, I think the furnace has gone out."

Sam nodded solemnly. "Grandma always says, when it rains, it pours."

"I think she was right," Maria muttered. "Except in this case, it floods."

Chapter Six

Maria sat in her bed with the remains of the Sunday paper spread around her. It wasn't really cold yet, so there wasn't any reason to panic. And there was the fireplace downstairs if it did get cold.

She'd tucked Sam in his bed with an extra blanket just to be sure. Then she'd called Mr. Spivey, who'd promised to be out the next morning to take a look at her furnace.

Like Billy, his words were ominous. "I think we talked last year about replacing that system, Mrs. Lightner. That thing's an antique!"

He'd chuckled at his joke, and Maria had groaned inwardly. The little bundle of money, safe in her bank account in Rockford, was rapidly dwindling. She knew she would not have any choice. She'd have to look for a job, at least until spring.

The paper was full of ads looking for everything from fry cooks to fire fighters. A few of the restaurants she knew were hiring waitresses but the money wouldn't pay for the trip into Rockford.

There was an ad, she saw it at once and circled it before she finished reading. Answering phones, dispatching cars, and the salary was great. When she reached the bottom of the ad, she sighed and crossed it out.

"Contact Sheriff Joe Roberts at the sheriff's office in Gold Springs."

She stared at it for a long time. He'd done what she had advised and put an ad in the paper. There were probably plenty of applicants. He might have already hired someone.

He hadn't mentioned the job that afternoon. Maybe he was hoping she wasn't considering it.

Not that she'd given him any reason to imagine she was considering it. She'd made her feelings plain on that subject. What was that old saying about burning bridges?

She looked at the ad again then put the paper away. Working in Gold Springs would be much better than working in Rockford. She turned out the light next to her bed. It was certainly more money.

Of course, the job might be taken already. And she would have to swallow a big gulp of pride to ask for it.

She closed her eyes in the darkened room, thinking about how much trouble she'd had the first year after Josh had died, sleeping alone in the big bed. But instead of seeing Josh's smiling face as she drifted off to sleep, Joe Roberts's face slid into her mind.

"Go to sleep," she told herself, thinking about his light touch on her hand.

But he followed her into her dreams, his strong arms

around her and his lips coming down on hers, blotting out the sun....

Then it was morning and the alarm was ringing and Sam was asking for cheese toast for breakfast, complaining that the house was cold.

The school bus came, and Mr. Spivey arrived at the same time the sheriff's car pulled into her driveway.

"Looks like you might be in trouble," Mr. Spivey joked as he took out his tools.

Maria looked regretfully at her old sweatpants and sweatshirt, her hair scraped from her face and held in place with a rubber band.

"I'll be looking at that old furnace of yours," Mr. Spivey promised. He stared at her, then at the sheriff as the other man got out of his car.

Maria smiled, knowing he wouldn't budge yet. Mr. Spivey was the biggest gossip in Gold Springs!

"Good morning," Mr. Spivey greeted the sheriff. "Out pretty early this morning."

Joe nodded and took the other man's extended hand. "On my way to the office."

"Crime doesn't sleep, I suppose," Mr. Spivey quipped.

Joe was looking at Maria. "Not in this town."

"Well," Mr. Spivey added, glancing between them, "I'll just go have a look at that furnace. You might want to come, too, Sheriff."

"Why's that, Mr. Spivey?"

"Might be the last time anyone ever sees one like it. I think they all died out in the last century. Mrs. Lightner's waited until last night."

Chuckling to himself, the repairman walked around the house.

Maria felt her toes curling with embarrassment inside her wet tennis shoes. If it wasn't Sam telling Joe Roberts her personal problems, it was the neighbors!

"Has your furnace died or is it just sick?" he wondered, looking into her bemused face.

She lifted one shoulder gracefully under the ragged sweatshirt. "We don't know yet, but Mr. Spivey is already planning the funeral service."

Joe laughed and longed to slide the sweatshirt fabric up her shoulder. Or was that slide it down?

"What brings you up this way, Sheriff?"

"I was going into town and I thought you might need a ride over to Billy's for your truck," he answered after a moment. He'd had difficulty recalling what it was that had brought him here after seeing her. She was like a cool drink on a hot day.

She looked purposely at her torn shoe, pride making her want to say no, thanks.

Pride that might eventually make her accept a ride with Tommy to Billy's garage. Pride lost out rapidly. "Thank you. It was nice of you to think of me."

Since thinking of her had become as natural to him as breathing, he grinned. "I enjoyed it."

She looked at him quickly, feeling color heat her cheeks. "I, uh, I have to change clothes, if you wouldn't mind waiting—"

"Not at all," he replied, his eyes caressing her gently. "I can wait."

"There's coffee." She invited him into the house. "If you don't mind the cold."

He nodded. "Coffee sounds good."

She chattered nervously about Sam and the truck she was picking up while she found a clean mug and filled it with hot coffee. There was something about him that morning that made her nervous. Or maybe it was that seeing him made her recall those dreams she'd had during the night.

Joe watched her movements as she ran around the kitchen, spilling the coffee and the sugar, almost pulling the silverware drawer out of the cabinet. There was something different about her. Or maybe it was remembering her touch yesterday.

"It's cold in here," she said, putting the mug on the table. She saw her own breath, frosty in the air between them, and frowned. "It won't take me long to change."

He sipped coffee as he heard her footsteps fly up the stairs. "Feels pretty warm in here to me," he murmured, letting his imagination go up the stairs with her.

"Well, she's dead, all right," Mr. Spivey said.

"Excuse me?" Joe choked on a swallow of coffee, his mind abruptly returning to the kitchen.

"The furnace, Sheriff. Mrs. Lightner's furnace is dead. I told her last year she needed a new system."

"How much?" Joe asked bluntly.

"Best I can do." Mr. Spivey quoted a high figure. "I can leave her a kerosene heater. Better than nothing until she can afford the new system."

He left his estimate on the table and promised to leave a heater on the porch.

Joe hated the forlorn look on Maria's face when she saw the quote Mr. Spivey had left for her. He wanted to step in and take care of it. Why should she and Sam be in a cold house for even one day?

But he knew Maria well enough to know she wouldn't thank him for the thought. They'd just reached speaking status again. He didn't want to do anything that would set them back.

If he could convince her to take the job at the sheriff's office…

"Well," she said, turning to him, "I'm ready, if you are."

The furnace repairs didn't come up. They talked about the Founder's Day celebration on the way to Billy's garage.

"Dennie and Mandy Lambert both asked me to escort them to the Founder's Dance this weekend," he told her with a chuckle.

"Watch out for them, Sheriff," Maria warned. "Don't let them get you in a dark corner."

Joe laughed. "It's the uniform. I'll wear something else Saturday night."

"I think you might be underestimating yourself," she retorted. "There aren't very many single men in this town who are under the age of sixty."

"Thank you, Ms. Lightner." He nodded without taking his eyes from the road. "You know how to keep a man from getting a big head."

They reached the garage quickly, too quickly for Maria, who found herself wishing they could spend a few more minutes together.

"I guess I'll see you around," she said as she got out of the car.

"If I don't see you before Saturday, I'll try to save you a dance," he promised.

She watched the car pull away before she ducked into the garage. The smell of grease and gasoline was overpowering.

"Billy?" she called.

"Back here," he yelled. "I've got it all ready to go for you, Maria."

She climbed into the truck and started it, reveling in the engine's purr. The truck wasn't fresh off a show-

FREE BOOKS! FREE GIFT!

PLAY BANGO!

AND CLAIM 2 FREE BOOKS AND A FREE GIFT!

BANGO

15	19	32	54	73
6	17	41	50	6
13	22	FREE	52	
5	24	44	46	
8	21	35	47	75

BANGO

9	19	44	52	71
4	20	32	50	68
11	18	FREE	53	63
7	27	36	60	72
3	28	41	47	64

★ **No Cost!**
★ **No Obligation to Buy!**
★ **No Purchase Necessary!**

TURN THE PAGE TO PLAY

PLAY BANGO!

AND GET THREE FREE GIFTS!

It looks like BINGO, it plays like BINGO but it's FREE!

HOW TO PLAY:

1. With a coin, scratch the Caller Card to reveal your 5 lucky numbers and see that they match your Bango Card. Then check the claim chart to discover what we have for you — FREE BOOKS and a FREE GIFT. All yours, all free!

2. Send back the Bango card and you'll receive 2 brand-new Silhouette Romance® novels. These books have a cover price of $3.50 each in the U.S. and $3.99 each in Canada, but they are yours to keep absolutely free.

3. There's no catch. You're under no obligation to buy anything. We charge nothing — ZERO — for your first shipment. And you don't have to make any minimum number of purchases — not even one!

4. The fact is, thousands of readers enjoy receiving books by mail from the Silhouette Reader Service® months before they are available in stores. They like the convenience of home delivery and they love our discount prices!

5. We hope that after receiving your free books you'll want to remain a subscriber. But the choice is yours — to continue or cancel, any time at all! So why not take us up on our invitation, with no risk of any kind. You'll be glad you did!

YOURS FREE!

This exciting mystery gift is yours free when you play BANGO!

It's fun, and we're giving away
FREE GIFTS
to all players!

The Silhouette Reader Service® — Here's how it works:

Accepting free books places you under no obligation to buy anything. You may keep the books and gift and return the shipping statement marked "cancel." If you do not cancel, about a month later we'll send you 6 additional novels and bill you just $2.90 each in the U.S., or $3.25 each in Canada, plus 25¢ delivery per book and applicable taxes if any.* That's the complete price — and compared to the cover price of $3.50 in the U.S. and $3.99 in Canada — it's quite a bargain! You may cancel at any time, but if you choose to continue, every month we'll send you 6 more books, which you may either purchase at the discount price or return to us and cancel your subscription.

*Terms and prices subject to change without notice. Sales tax applicable in N.Y. Canadian residents will be charged applicable provincial taxes and GST.

BUSINESS REPLY MAIL
FIRST-CLASS MAIL   PERMIT NO. 717   BUFFALO, NY

POSTAGE WILL BE PAID BY ADDRESSEE

SILHOUETTE READER SERVICE
3010 WALDEN AVE
PO BOX 1867
BUFFALO NY 14240-9952

NO POSTAGE
NECESSARY
IF MAILED
IN THE
UNITED STATES

If offer card is missing write to: Silhouette Reader Service, 3010 Walden Ave., P.O. Box 1867, Buffalo, NY 14240-1867 room floor, but it was clean and years newer than the one that had died.

"Weekly payments, right?" Billy asked as he closed the hood.

"Weekly payments," she agreed with a tense nod. "Thanks, Billy."

"No problem, Maria. See you Friday."

Friday, she mused, driving her new black truck home. Her first payment day.

The estimate Mr. Spivey had left had made her gasp. Not that she was surprised. For the past two years, she had barely been able to keep them going. There was very little left over for major upkeep or new purchases.

She looked at herself in the bedroom mirror and came to a decision. Maybe he'd laugh or maybe he'd already hired someone for the job, but she was going to ask for it anyway. With the added expenses of the furnace and the truck, she would never make it to the next harvest with what she'd saved.

Maybe, she told herself optimistically as she dressed, she could even afford that computer for Sam, after all.

She refused to consider what she would say if the job was already taken. But she wasn't going to let pride stand in her way.

An hour later, every hair in place, for once, her cranberry red suit perfectly creased, white blouse a smooth contrast, she walked into the sheriff's office.

Painters were working all over the building alongside carpenters, who were repairing years of damage. An electrician hung from a ladder rewiring the lights in the ceiling.

"Is the sheriff here?" she asked.

No one answered. She raised her voice a little, but there was still no answer.

Finally, she put her hands on her hips and adjusted her voice to the tone she used to call Sam home for supper. "Is the sheriff here?"

The work ceased abruptly, and her words echoed through the old city hall.

"Is there something I can do for you, Ms. Lightner?" Joe questioned, stepping out of a side door.

His tone was cool but his eyes felt warm on her as she walked across the old wooden floor in her best black heels. Nervous as she'd been the first time she went out to look for a job, she held her shoulders back and her head up even though her insides were churning.

"I've come about the job," she told him, locking her gaze with his as she approached him.

Joe looked around at the suddenly quiet workmen, and the noise resumed as though it had never stopped. Interested eyes watched them intently to report back to wives and sisters what they had seen, but the hammers and brushes didn't miss another beat.

"What job is that?" he wondered, his face a careful blank.

"This job." She handed him the paper with the want ad crossed out.

He studied her awkwardly then relented. "Come in my office."

His "office" was really a large storage closet that had been converted into a shelter from the dust and noise of the remodeling. He offered her a chair and took one himself on the other side of the battered old desk that was piled high with papers.

He glanced at the newspaper. "It looks as though you weren't interested in this ad."

"I wasn't," she answered truthfully, "at first."

"What made you change your mind?"

She glared at him, shuffling her feet uneasily. How hard did he plan to make this? "I, uh, thought about how close it would be to my home and that the pay was better than I could get in Rockford."

"So, you were willing to make a sacrifice in your working conditions?" he queried.

Maria looked at him in his uniform with his arresting dark looks, his long hands holding the piece of newspaper she'd handed him. "I think I can handle whatever comes up."

"That's great." He nodded. "You're hired."

"But you don't even know my qualifications," she protested.

He came around the desk and sat on the edge. "You're the only person in this town who has any idea how to handle an emergency call. You were the sheriff's wife. You heard it all. The system is easy to learn. Once the switchboard is put in here, you'll train others to take the calls."

"I do some typing," she told him, improvising. "I can figure out a few computer programs."

There was a shout and some cursing from the other room followed by a call on the radio from one of the deputies.

"Can you handle work crews, as well?" he asked, going to the radio to answer.

"I think so. I—"

"Sheriff Roberts, there's a mess down here at the general store, and we're not sure what to do." The worried voice of a first-time deputy came through on the radio.

"I'll be there in a few minutes," Joe replied, his voice a calm contrast to the deputy's. "Can you start right now?'' he asked Maria, not missing a step as he grabbed his hat and headed for the door.

She nodded. "Sure. I suppose I—"

"You're it, then," he told her briefly, and went out.

She stood slowly, perusing the mess, wondering where to start.

"Oh," Joe said, poking his head around the door frame, "thanks, Maria."

He smiled quickly and was gone, but she felt a flash zoom from her toes to her chest. There was another loud thud from the main area followed by a chorus of angry voices.

"I think I know where to start," she said, leaving the paperwork until later.

Joe climbed into the patrol car and started toward the store on the edge of town. Probably a couple of hotheads who didn't know when to go home.

He thought about Maria, elated she had decided to take the job. Seeing her standing there in the doorway, that red suit hugging her slender form, it was a struggle to remain coherent when she smiled at him. Her gaze grabbed his and wouldn't let go.

After he had worked through the problem at the general store, he would go past Spivey's Heating and Air-Conditioning. He couldn't let a new employee of the sheriff's department cope with a cold house.

Warm homes meant better employees, he thought, stopping the car at the general store. They could deduct an amount from her salary each week.

He was making it too personal. But there didn't seem to be any other answer. Maria had become a little more important than he'd thought possible. He hadn't planned on that kind of involvement, certainly hadn't looked for it. Yet there she was with those flashing blue eyes and that sweet mouth.

If he and Rachel had made it and they'd had a son like Sam, he hoped someone would have helped his family if he couldn't be there. He thought about Josh Lightner and hoped he and Josh were as much alike as they seemed and that he would understand.

He opened the patrol car door, and a shot rang out from inside the store.

By lunchtime, Maria had lost her suit jacket and the clip that had held her hair in place.

But the workmen were convinced the job needed to be done as quickly as possible, and the painters had been sent home until the electrician and the carpenters were through with their part. She had convinced the carpenter to bring in more crew by promising him he wouldn't see another paycheck until the work was done.

Then she'd started to work on Joe's desk. There was a banged-up file cabinet in a dusty corner, but it was empty. All the files he had collected since he'd come to Gold Springs were laying on and around his desk.

Groups of papers were spread out on the floor and across a side table that was covered with maps of the area.

Slowly, one file at a time, Maria began to make headway in clearing off the desk. She started her own filing system to keep track of the information, writing everything down so the sheriff could find it, as well.

There was a file on the Lightner family and a separate file on Josh, which she opened and scanned quickly with an anxious eye on the door. It wasn't much. A few words from the county about Josh's death and the investigation.

There was a note attached to a fax that gave Frank Martin's possible release date as the end of the next year. There was a warning, as well, about possible problems if Frank Martin decided to come back to Gold Springs.

Maria looked at the date. Joe had received the information last week. She closed the file quickly and put it with the others.

They were right. The information that Frank Martin was going to be released wouldn't be welcomed by the Lightner family. She had mixed feelings herself.

The door opened, and she jumped, feeling guilty that she had read the files. Joe and two deputies walked into the office, still talking excitedly about the call at the general store.

"I was scared," a young, thin man with short brown hair said. "When that gun went off…whew!"

Another man Maria recognized from the gas station just outside Gold Springs, though she didn't know his name. He was clapping the young man on the back.

"You handled it pretty well. I couldn't believe when the sheriff just walked right by you and asked Ray for the gun! That took some—" He stopped and squinted at Maria.

Joe saw the color drain from Maria's face. He ushered the two men out of his office and closed the door behind them. "Are you okay?"

She nodded, pulling herself together. "I've been filing."

"Filing," Joe repeated enthusiastically. "It looks great so far."

"I saw the file on Frank Martin," she admitted honestly. "I saw his parole date."

Joe sat in his chair, lacing his fingers together as he looked out the dirty window. "There's going to be some things in this office that aren't public knowledge. The Lightner family's attorneys will be notified of the date next week. In the meantime—" his voice changed as his gaze swung to her "—the information is privileged."

She nodded, looking at the desktop, which was dusty but visible. "I know."

"I wouldn't have wanted you here if I didn't feel I could trust you, Maria," he told her solemnly. "This is a hard one for you, personally, but there will be others. If you feel like that's too much to ask…"

"I don't," she replied quickly, raising her head. "I can handle it. What about the shooting?"

"It was Ray Morrison. There wasn't actually a shooting. More a misunderstanding."

She was unimpressed. "Someone misunderstood a gun?"

"Ray was trying out a gun at the store, and it went off. J.P. tried to tell him that he couldn't try it out inside, but Ray was drunk and wouldn't listen."

"So you walked up and asked for the gun," she guessed.

"There wasn't much else I could do." He wanted her to understand. He wanted her to be able to live with it.

Maria held her hands tightly together, feeling them tremble. "I sent the painters home until the carpenters and electricians are done. They were just getting in each other's way and—"

"Maria." He hesitated, then plunged forward. "I'm not Josh."

"I didn't think you were." She didn't want to think, just then, how she felt about it. She just wanted to get through the day.

"I've had twenty years of experience and constant training. Nothing is going to happen."

She leveled him with a painful stare. "Josh told me the same thing every time he walked out our front door."

There was nothing else to say. Joe laid his hat on the desk as she left. Words alone would never convince Maria that life didn't always repeat itself.

And why should she be convinced, after all? To set herself and Sam up to be hurt again? No one had the right to ask that from another human being.

Their working relationship was the same for the next few days. Mostly they avoided each other, and when they did see one another, their words were always to the point and always about the office.

It only took the first two days to straighten the office and start the process of cataloguing and organizing the old furniture that had been left in the city hall. Maria laid out a floor plan of the five offices and the entranceway and left it on Joe's desk.

She left at five, making a note to call the painters the following day. The carpenter and his crew were nearly finished with the repairs. The electrician had finished that day and had left Maria his invoice. She'd left that for Joe, as well, knowing he would be the one responsible for sending it on to the county.

The emergency system equipment would be installed at the end of the month, along with computers and other electronics. Joe had left her a note that he wanted her to put an ad in the paper for more help. He would leave it to her to interview and choose the candidates she thought were right.

She hadn't seen him all day. He'd been at meetings with the county commission in Rockford. She'd fielded calls for him and answered questions. The office was mostly quiet and strangely empty.

Maria tried not to think about his absence. If she never got attached to him, she wouldn't miss him if something happened. He was the sheriff. She worked at the sheriff's office. It never needed to go beyond that.

Sam was out of school before she was home from work. They decided he would get off the school bus at the Lightner house and she would pick him up there in the evening.

He showed her the start of a wooden sculpture he was learning to make with his grandfather's help while he was waiting for her each afternoon.

"It's a duck," he told her, holding it up proudly.

Glad he hadn't asked her to guess what it was, she smiled. "That's really good. How was school today?"

"Okay, I guess. They want us to put on some play for Christmas this year. Something with angels and sheep. Like they do at the church every year."

"That sounds nice," she replied. "Don't you think so?"

"I don't want to be a sheep," he confessed. "I didn't want to be in the dumb play at all but I really don't want to be a sheep."

"I guess everybody has to be something. Not everyone can be the good stuff."

He shrugged and settled his book bag. "I guess. What's for supper?"

She went over their supply of food in her mind. "We can have potpies or we can have pizza. Either one we can use the oven, and the kitchen will be warmer, too."

"Can we have French fries with the potpies?"

She nodded. "Sure."

"When are we going to get the furnace fixed? It's getting pretty cold."

Maria watched him draw a picture on the truck window with his warm breath and his finger. "Soon, I hope."

Actually, she wasn't sure when they would be able to save the cash. She'd tried to get a loan but she wasn't a good risk. She could ask the Lightners, but she hated to do that.

She pulled the truck into the yard and looked at Sam.

"Let's start a fire in the fireplace and eat in there. It'll be warmer than the kitchen table for your homework, too."

"Do I have to bring in wood?" Sam added, groaning.

"I'll start supper and help you," she suggested.

"Okay."

They went inside and Sam put his books on the kitchen table. "Feels warm in here."

Maria nodded. A faint hope that the old furnace might have kicked on, that it wasn't dead after all, crept in. It wasn't possible, but all the same, there was warm air coming from the vent.

"There's heat," Sam rejoiced. "We can have something for supper that's not frozen!"

Maria frowned. "Maybe Mr. Spivey was able to fix it."

She dialed the repairman's number and asked him, when he answered, if he had fixed her furnace.

"That's a good one, Mrs. Lightner!" He hooted. "As if that thing could be fixed."

"Well, it's running," she explained, annoyed.

"That's the new furnace! Should be good for twenty years. Feels good, huh?"

Maria considered his words. "But, Mr. Spivey, I didn't pay for the new furnace to be put in."

"That's true enough. But the sheriff's money is as good as yours, Mrs. Lightner."

"The sheriff?" she demanded, a sinking feeling in the pit of her stomach.

"He came by and paid for the new system a few days ago. He must've forgot to tell you."

"He must have," she agreed blankly. "Thanks, Mr. Spivey."

Maria tried to reach Joe at the office while Sam was doing his homework, but there was no answer. She found it hard to believe that a man who barely knew her would have a new furnace put in her house.

Just as she thought everything was going to be all right, too. That was the hard part. She had thought she would be able to afford the furnace after a while. Now she would have the embarrassment of having to tell Mr. Spivey to take the system out or borrow the money from the Lightners to pay off Joe Roberts.

How could he do such a thing? she wondered, pacing the warm floor in the middle of the night. Sometime before dawn, she decided he wanted something in return and that was his way of getting it. The warm looks, the kiss in her kitchen. He was no better than Tommy Lightner!

Chapter Seven

The following morning she was in the office early, to be sure that she didn't miss Joe. Her resignation was in her purse.

She walked under the new sign, admiring the work Doug Ruggles had done on it. Gold Springs was coming around slowly to the new sheriff, even if he was an outsider.

"Hello?" she called, anger pushing her dragging feet and spirits into the building.

The silence in the old building was unnerving. She was about to leave and wait for him in the street when the double doors were flung open and all hell broke loose.

"You won't be able to keep me here," Ricky Lightner yelled as he fought with the two deputies who were walking him into the building.

"Settle down," Joe advised him, following them in, closing the doors. "Take a chair, Ricky."

"My parents will be here with our lawyer," Ricky

threatened, still trying to shrug off the deputies even though his hands were in cuffs. His young face was cut in a few places, nothing that looked serious, but Maria went for the first aid kit.

"I'm glad you're here," Joe told her quietly when she returned.

She nodded, angry that she would have to wait. "What is Ricky doing here?"

"He was racing with his buddies at the crossroads again," the sheriff explained briefly. "Scratched himself up wrapping his car around a tree."

The two deputies left to go bring in the rest of the drivers. Two more were coming in with the other patrol car.

"Get their names," Joe instructed Maria. "We'll call their parents from here, and they can come and get them."

"What are you doing here, Maria?" Ricky asked her as she opened the first aid kit on the desk.

"I'm working here," she explained, taking out a cotton swab and some Betadine. "Hold still, and I'll clean those cuts for you."

"Working here?" He laughed angrily. "Don't expect to for long! You know Mom will close this place down over this!"

"You can't close down a sheriff's office just because you don't like what they do," Maria told him patiently. "When you break the law—"

"The law is what we say it is," Ricky told her, jerking his face away from her touch. "She won't thank you for being here, either, you know."

"I know," she admitted.

The Lightners walked through the front doors as the second group of boys were being brought in from the patrol cars. Joel and Anna saw Ricky and stalked to his side.

"What is going on here?" Anna demanded, then caught sight of Maria as she was calling the other boys' parents. "Maria! Are you a part of this?"

"Mrs. Lightner, Mr. Lightner." Joe spoke, drawing their attention. His dark face was carefully composed.

"Sheriff." Joel nodded. "What's happened?"

"I had to pick your son up for racing at the crossroads. We've given the boys plenty of warnings, and they ignored us."

"Well, no wonder." Anna Lightner mocked him, her silver-blond head held high. "Boys have been racing there since I was a little girl. You can't just breeze into town and stop it."

Joe stared at her. "What your son has been doing is against the state and county laws, Mrs. Lightner. Maybe in your day, it wasn't. Today, the county wants it stopped."

"That's ridiculous!"

"Anna." Her husband tried to hush her.

"Our lawyer will be here shortly," she continued, disregarding him.

"I haven't arrested Ricky," Joe told her flatly. "I wanted to be sure all the boys' parents were aware of what was happening. The boys are minors, but the next time, they will spend a night in the county jail."

"We appreciate the warning." Joel thanked him, taking his hand. "Can we take the boy home now?"

"Sure," Joe replied. "We'll be keeping his car, what's left of it, for three days. He can pick it up then."

"You'll regret this decision," Anna added acidly. "Let's go home, Ricky."

Other parents were arriving in varying states of anger

and hostility. Some of the mothers were crying. A few of the fathers were shouting at both the sheriff and their sons.

Maria watched from the desk. Joe never raised his voice, calmly explaining what had happened and what would happen if the boys were caught again. His usually expressive face was bland, but the eyes were watchful. She had the feeling that if any of the fathers had done more than shout, he would have been ready for it.

Maria realized there was a difference between Joe and Josh.

Josh had been a truly easygoing spirit, tripping through his good deeds like a big Boy Scout earning merit badges.

Joe was harder, more determined. A part of him waited and watched until he saw the problem. He was more a soldier doing his job and less a scout doing good deeds, even though he seemed to spend his time looking out for others.

Which brought her to her own problem. The last parents were leaving, and the yawning deputies were going for coffee.

E.J. Marks, a deputy and a well driller who'd put in Maria's well, nodded to her courteously. He looked dressed up in his uniform. "Would you like to come with us, Mrs. Lightner?"

"No, thanks, E.J.," she responded quietly, wishing he would leave so she could get on with it.

"Sheriff?" He looked at the man behind her, respect and something approaching friendship in his pale blue eyes.

"No, thanks, E.J. Maybe later." Joe sat on the dusty hulk of an old desk in the entryway.

E.J. nodded and left.

"Okay," Joe said. "I'm here. A willing target."

"What do you mean?" Maria asked nervously. "Are you a mind reader now?"

He smiled at her, and she looked away. "It doesn't take much mind reading to know that Mr. Spivey finally got around to your furnace and then ratted me out."

"What were you thinking?" she demanded, her hands held tightly together in front of her.

"I was thinking that there was no reason for you and Sam to suffer. You're working for me. We can work out a payment plan."

She stared at him furiously. "And what sort of payment plan did you have in mind?"

"The kind where you pay what you can afford every week or two until it's paid for," he said slowly, his eyes never leaving hers. "What sort did you have in mind, Maria?"

She felt strangely elated but refused to allow her light-headedness to make her giddy. "We've been...well, you kissed me."

"And you kissed me," he countered.

"I thought you might want more." She spelled it out for him uncomfortably.

His gaze never wavered. "I do. Want more, that is. But I hope I haven't come to a place in my life when I have to blackmail a woman to have a relationship with her."

"So," she continued, trying to find her way out of a difficult situation. She had pushed them beyond their employer-employee relationship. Struggling furiously to get back, she searched for words.

"So." He stood up and dusted off his pants with a careless hand. "We can get back to work?"

She nodded, relieved. "Did you have a chance to look over those perspectives on the building?"

"I did," he agreed. "I'll have to have the okay from the commission but I thought they looked pretty good."

"Good," she answered, suddenly shy. "I'll, uh, get going on something else."

He nodded. "You'll need to give the county offices a call and set up your schedule to start training before the emergency equipment gets here."

"All right."

He leaned close to her and smiled. "I put that note on your desk, Mrs. Lightner."

"Thanks," she whispered, trying to catch her breath.

She didn't see him again that morning, and she spent the time wisely, reminding herself that she wasn't a teenager anymore. A man coming close to her couldn't take her breath away.

Being around Joe was like being too close to an electrical current. The fine hairs on the back of her neck whispered against her skin, and she could feel a tingling in her fingers and toes.

She laughed at herself, feeling young and foolish. She wasn't either, of course. She was a staid widow with a young son and responsibilities.

Yet there was a part of her that wanted to feel silly and lighthearted again. It had been so long since she'd felt that way. Just the thought of it made her feel fear and guilt.

What if Joe wasn't interested in anything more than a fast affair? She didn't think she could feel quite that young and silly.

Yet how could she fall in love with Joe when she had promised to love Josh forever? And even though Joe was different, there was still the very real danger that they could ultimately suffer the same fate.

It was five minutes to five when she looked at the clock directly across from her desk. She'd claimed the desk and a chair from the stock in the storage area. She'd used spray polish on them until they gleamed, then she'd turned her rag on Joe's desk and chair.

Would he notice? she wondered, looking at them in the last motes of dying sunlight.

She picked up her coat and purse and closed the office door behind her. The outer area, which would eventually be a hub of activity, was still full of sawdust and short pieces of wire.

The carpentry crew had finished that day, and the painters were due after the weekend. The office would be ready for the new equipment, as well as the new employees.

Maria felt a strong satisfaction about making everything work together, even arguing with the painters. Taking the raw remains of the old city hall and making it into a shining new sheriff's office appealed to her sense of order. It was different than her herb-growing business and could never take its place, but she liked it.

A light was on in one of the unused areas in the back, and she turned away, planning to leave as though she hadn't seen it. She was tired, and Sam was waiting for her.

But she'd turned off too many lights in her home, following Sam's trail through the house. With a sigh, she turned and waded through the piles of furniture and gallons of paint to reach the tiny room.

Standing on the tips of her toes to reach the cord that came down from the naked lightbulb, Maria put all her weight on one floorboard.

Without warning, the narrow plank under her foot gave way, and she pitched forward. She caught herself on the palms of her hands, but not before she scraped her right knee. What was worse was that her foot was wedged into the hole in the floorboard, and no matter what she tried, she couldn't get it free.

For a few long moments, she pulled and pried, but the shoe and her foot were firmly inserted into the wood.

Maria looked around for some tools to use on the old wood. Long strings of curses ribboned through her brain, and she heartily planned on recalling them on Monday when she saw the carpenter and his crew. They had assured her that all the floors were safe.

Her hand fell on a paint scraper, but it was as useless as her own two hands had been. Her palms were stinging, and her knee was cut and bleeding. She sat on the floor and tried to get her foot out of her shoe.

She refused to give in to her fears that she might spend the night in that dirty little room, glad she hadn't been able to reach the light cord. At least she wasn't sitting in the dark, worrying about hearing scurrying noises, wondering if there were rats.

A scraping behind one of the old desks caught her ear, and she felt her stomach tighten. It probably was rats, but she had faced them in barns since she was a little girl. Of course, she hadn't been trapped with her foot in the floor.

She didn't know how long it had been but she was hurt and tired. She felt herself start to nod off after a while and sat up straighter, glancing at her watch. She had been trapped with her foot in the floor for over two hours.

Surely Anna would be wondering why she hadn't come to pick up Sam. Maybe she would call the sheriff or one of the deputies, and one of them would come to look for her.

She heard the front doors open and close. "Hello? Hello? Is someone out there?"

"Maria?" came the quick reply.

"Joe," she called eagerly. "I'm back here. Bring a hammer or something with you."

"What's happened? Maria?"

"I'm back here." She hated that her voice sounded tearful, but she was very glad that he'd come. "Back here with the light."

"Maria?" He glanced into the little room and saw her sitting on the floor.

"Joe," she answered, wiping a dirty hand across her eyes, trying to keep him from seeing that she was crying.

"What are you doing back here? Are you all right?"

"I came to turn off the light that those damn carpenters left on, and the floor gave way. My foot is stuck."

He knelt at her side, looking at her foot and the hole in the floor. "How long have you been back here?"

"About two hours," she replied, thankful to see his handsome face. Although she had to admit she would have been happy to see any face.

"Let me get a crowbar out of the truck, and I'll have you out in a second. This wood is rotten. It's the way your foot is wedged in that makes it so tough to get out."

"Okay," she agreed weakly.

He heard the tremor in her voice and looked at her, wishing he had the carpenter in his hands at that moment. "It's going to be okay," he told her. "I'll be right back."

Maria waited impatiently, the few short moments he was gone seeming like several hours.

He came back with the crowbar and dug the sharp end into the rotted wood. "Try pulling."

Maria tried to get her foot out, but it was no use. "I don't know if it's coming out. I might have to live here."

"I don't think so," he responded, putting the crowbar into the wood. The rotted wood splintered and broke under the steady pressure.

Maria pulled her foot out, feeling better at once. "Thank you, thank you," she said again and again, more relieved than she realized.

He helped her to her feet, and she clung tightly to him. He couldn't fight the feel of her in his arms, wouldn't even try. The best he could do was hold on tightly, closing his eyes and letting the sweet smell of her perfume encompass him.

"I don't know if I can walk," she said finally, sniffing a little. "My foot is numb."

Without a word, he caught her up in his arms, looking closely into her tearstained face.

"I didn't mean you had to carry me," she said, her voice catching on a sob.

"No problem," he whispered, his mouth brushing hers lightly.

Maria felt her lips part in anticipation. His eyes were so dark. Tiny laugh lines fanned out on the sides. She looked at his lips, and her eyes closed, wanting more.

Barely grazing her temple, his lips moved to her

cheekbone and drifted to each eyelid. By the time he reached her lips, she was eager for the hard pressure, the inviting heat he conveyed to her.

She felt him move, leaning against a desk, adjusting her so she was snuggled more fully into his chest and lap. She didn't care. She wanted him closer and wrapped her arms around his neck, sliding her fingers through his thick hair.

"Maria," he whispered, so close to her ear that his breath tickled and she shivered. His tongue touched the shell of her ear, and she squirmed in his lap, making them both aware of how much he wanted her.

Maria kissed the spot at the base of his throat where his shirt was open and wished she could undo the rest of the buttons. She wanted to touch him, to feel him move under her hands—

"I hope you're not just trying to get out of making those weekly payments," he whispered with a rich chuckle.

"I'm sorry," she said primly. "I thought that you'd try to take advantage of me."

"Give me a chance," he said, kissing the side of her neck. "I'd love to take advantage of you."

"I didn't mean that." She sighed, almost forgetting what she did mean when she felt his hand on her thigh.

She jumped and bit her lip when his hand grazed her cut knee.

"Sorry," he apologized, kissing her once more quickly before standing up. "I think we'd better take care of those cuts and scratches, ma'am, before I take advantage of you any further."

"Why, thank you, Sheriff," she drawled in her most charming southern lady voice, fluttering her eyelashes at him. "I appreciate your consideration."

He sat her in a straight-back wooden chair and knelt at her feet after grabbing the first aid kit from the storage shelf.

"This doesn't look too bad," he said. Carefully, he cut away the thin hose from her knee and cleaned the narrow gash. Then he applied anti-infection cream and covered it with a Band-Aid.

"That feels better," she admitted, aware of how alone they were in the big old building.

"Let's check your foot," he said, smiling at her before he removed her battered shoe. "I think someone owes you a new pair of shoes."

"As long as I don't need a new foot, you won't hear me complaining." She wiggled her toes experimentally.

"Everything seems to be okay. But I'll run you to the hospital if you think—"

"No," she answered, shaking her head. "I'll be fine."

"You should probably go home and put some ice on that," he observed.

Maria's eyes widened. "Sam! I forgot all about Sam."

He brought her a phone and went to look over his messages while she called her in-laws. When he thought about her being trapped all weekend, it made him shudder. Thank God she hadn't been more seriously injured.

All the same, he had a few choice words for the man who was responsible for giving them the all clear on the floor. The accident wasn't serious, but it could have been.

"I'm going to pick up Sam," she called to him.

Joe met her at the door. "I don't think so. What if

your injury is more serious than we think it is? What if you drive off and get into an accident and you and Sam are hurt?''

She smiled slowly. "What did you have in mind?"

"I'm going to drive you home. I'll bring you back tomorrow to pick up your truck. I couldn't sleep tonight knowing I let you drive with an injured foot."

"I'll be fine, Joe, really."

"I wouldn't be doing my job if I let a driver go out on the road in less than perfect condition," he explained.

"All right," she agreed. Her knee still hurt, and she was tired and eager to get home. She could tell from Sam's voice on the phone that he was anxious about her, as well. "You can drive me home."

He grinned, helping her with her coat and purse. "Like you had a choice."

"I think I could have hobbled to the door faster than you realize," she quipped.

He scooped her up in his arms and started for the door.

"You don't have to carry me," she told him.

"Stopped you from hobbling anywhere, didn't it?" he asked. "Besides, I like the way it feels."

She was quiet while he put her in the patrol car and fussed over her. It was nice having someone look after her for a change. It had been a long time.

"I suppose I'll have to ask you in for supper since you're taking me home," she said with a sigh as he started the car.

"I wouldn't want to impose," he demurred. But when Sam got into the patrol car, the first thing he did was invite the sheriff home for supper.

"Your mother has a hurt foot and knee," Joe told him. "We'd have to cook whatever we eat."

"We could do that," the boy said. "We have plenty of frozen food."

It was decided. Maria sat and listened while the two of them talked about what they'd done that day.

Is that what Josh would have wanted? she found herself wondering as she looked into the night. Would he have wanted his son to have a second chance for a father?

When they reached the house, Joe picked her up and Sam opened the door. Like a queen ensconced on her throne, Maria sat while they took her coat and Sam fetched her slippers.

"You'll have to sit in the kitchen," Sam explained carefully as though she might have a hard time understanding. "We might need your help."

"That's fine," she replied, touching his face lightly. "What are you going to make for supper?"

Sam showed Joe around the old-fashioned kitchen. They surveyed the contents of the cabinets then checked out the freezer.

Maria sat with a cup of herb tea and watched as they spread ingredients on the counter. Joe set Sam on a stool at the counter and had him peel potatoes. He took down her largest cast-iron frying pan with a grace and ease she envied, landing it on the stove with a gentle slide.

"What do we call this?" Maria asked as he started to add ingredients.

"We call this hash," he responded, throwing in onions after the potatoes. "In Toledo, it's Toledo hash. In Dallas, it's Texas hash."

"How about in Gold Springs?" she asked, laughing.

"Here," he answered with a smile in her direction, "we call it Maria's hash."

"Can't it be Sam's hash?" Sam demanded.

Joe frowned at him. "Your mother has a hurt foot. That's why we're making it. That's why we have to call it Maria's hash."

"Okay." Sam considered his words. "I'll get the plates and glasses.

The kitchen was fragrant with frying ingredients, including many of Maria's fresh herbs, which she'd never used in this way. When the hash was finished, Joe heaped it on the plates.

"Great!" Sam complimented as he tasted his dinner.

"It's really good," Maria added, impressed. Of course, Joe would have to be able to cook for himself. He'd lived alone most of his life.

Not that she could imagine he'd been without some female companionship in his life. Had there ever been someone serious?

"Hot chocolate, anyone?" Joe asked when they were finished eating.

"Let's have it by the fire," Sam suggested. "We could tell ghost stories like they do on Founder's Day."

"Ghost stories," Joe repeated seriously. "I didn't know that was part of Founder's Day."

Maria looked at Sam, and the two of them laughed. "You have a surprise coming, then. Founder's Day is based on ghost stories."

Sitting in front of the fire that took a little coaxing to roar in the stone hearth, Maria held her cup carefully while Sam started to tell his story.

"Gold Springs was a mining town to begin with," he said in his scariest voice. "People came here from all across the country when they heard about the big gold strike. Lots of them were mean and lots of them were running away from the law in other places.

"Two brothers came here with hardly the clothes on their back and they started to dig 'cause that's what you had to do. One brother hit a lucky streak right away and his shovel was full of gold. The other brother couldn't find any gold no matter how hard he tried.

"So the brother that couldn't find any hated the brother that could. He knew that lots of people had dug lots of holes all over the place looking for gold, and he got an idea. He covered up one of the deepest holes with a thin piece of tar paper and spread some leaves over the top. Then he called his brother.

"When his brother came, the bad brother told him he had seen something across where the hole was in a clearing. His brother didn't know what was going on and he walked right over that hole and sank into the shaft and was never seen…alive…again."

"We have a habit of falling into things in this town," Maria said, mocking herself.

"So what happened next?" Joe asked the boy.

"Well," Sam elaborated, "they say that almost right away, folks started to see the dead brother. He appeared in front of a few miners in the saloon, but when they tried to talk to him, he disappeared. People began to say one brother had killed the other one and taken his gold.

"Of course, they were right. The brother that was alive was having a good time with the dead brother's gold, living in his house, dancing with pretty women in the saloon until dawn.

"Then one night when he'd been out really late, the brother was on his way home, and he heard something in the woods. He went to see what it was and saw a lantern swaying in the wind hanging on a tree limb.

"He tried to reach for it, but he didn't notice there was an open shaft, and he fell down in it, even farther than his brother.

"Folks said that the ghost of his brother tricked him into falling with that lantern. And today, some folks say you can still hear them arguing in the woods late at night. A lantern appears on a tree limb and then there's no more sounds. The brothers each got their revenge."

"Whew!" Joe sat back and took a sip from his cup. "That was pretty intense. Where did you hear that story?"

"They tell it every year at Founder's Day," Sam replied as though it was nothing. "Mom said they told it every year when she was a kid, too."

"That's true," Maria agreed. "That one and a few others. Gold Springs is full of ghosts."

"And open holes that people fall into?" Joe asked sarcastically.

Maria nodded solemnly. "People from Gold Springs have a hard time knowing how to put one foot in front of another. We're good at preserving the past but we're scared of the future."

Joe studied her profile in the firelight. "That's why you need some outside blood here. So someone can drag you kicking and screaming into the future."

"Is that why you're here?" Maria asked seriously.

He nodded. "It seems that way to me."

Chapter Eight

The fire had begun to burn down, and the hot chocolate was gone.

"It's getting late." Maria was the first to make a move. She was tired, and her foot and leg were throbbing painfully.

"That's true," Joe acknowledged, taking his cue to get to his feet. He carefully closed the glass doors on the fireplace while Sam took their cups to the kitchen.

"I guess you know what to expect from Founder's Day now," she said nervously. "It's kind of a strange mixture of ghosts and parades and barbecues."

He laughed. "What about the dance tomorrow night? Are you leaving me to the wolves?"

"I don't think I'm going to be in much shape to dance," she retorted, "but since the dance begins Founder's Week, I have to go."

"How about if I pick you up tomorrow night for the dance and I can drop you off at your truck afterward?"

"All right," she answered, swallowing hard and smiling. "That would be fine."

"I'll call you in the morning about the time," he promised.

She nodded. "Okay."

He stepped closer to her, offering his hand to help her from the chair. Maria took a deep breath and felt his hand close around hers, warm and real.

"Are you leaving, Joe?" Sam asked, coming in from the kitchen.

"Yeah," he replied, his glance at Maria full of unspoken regrets. "It's been a long day. I have early patrol tomorrow."

"I'd like to be a deputy," Sam told him.

Joe nodded. "You'll have to finish school first," he told the boy. "But it's something to work for."

Sam agreed. "I want to be a hero like my dad."

Maria drew a ragged breath. "I thought you wanted to build computers, Sam."

"Maybe." He considered. "If not, maybe I'll be a race car driver."

Maria smiled and tousled her son's hair. "You've got a long time to decide."

"Your mom's right, Sam," Joe added. "The whole world's in front of you."

"Are you and Mom going to the dance tomorrow?" he asked, looking at the two of them.

"Maybe," Maria admitted with a glance at Joe.

"Great," the boy said. "We'll see you tomorrow."

"Bet on it," Joe replied. "I guess I'll call it a night. Thanks for dinner."

"We were glad to have you, weren't we, Mom?"

"Yes, we were. I appreciate the lift home, Sheriff."

"You can call him Joe," Sam reminded her. "We knew him before he was the sheriff, remember?"

"I remember, Sam," Maria assured him.

"Tomorrow then," Joe said.

"We'll see you," Sam said cheerfully.

When Joe had gone and the porch light was off, Maria started hobbling toward the stairs.

"He's a great guy," Sam said, skipping around her. "I think you should go to the dance with him."

"I think you shouldn't worry about who I go to the dance with," she retorted. "Who are you taking to the dance?"

Sam made a face. "I'm not going, remember? Uncle Pete is taking me and Grandma fishing for the whole day and night. I don't want to go anywhere near where a bunch of people are dancing."

She laughed. "That's what I thought. Why do you want me to go?"

"Because Joe's a nice guy. And I think he likes you."

Maria felt her face turn red. "I think we should both go to bed, Sam. Think you can tuck yourself in?"

He took her hand. "I want to tuck you in for a change," he told her quietly. "You need my help tonight."

While Maria changed into her nightgown, Sam pulled back her blanket and fluffed her pillow.

"Do you need a drink of water?" he asked her solemnly when she'd climbed under the covers.

Maria looked into his sweet face and nodded. "I am a little thirsty."

Mimicking her moves every night since he'd been born, he went and filled a small glass halfway with water and put it on the bedside table after she'd taken a sip.

"Go right to sleep," he told her, kissing her forehead. "I love you and I'll see you in the morning."

"I love you, too, Sam," Maria whispered through a tight throat. "I'll see you in the morning."

"Good night, Mom."

She'd done it, Maria told herself as she drifted close to sleep. After all the times she'd said no, she'd finally accepted a date with a man.

The next morning, the repercussions attacked her.

Maria went over what was said between them. Had Joe really meant they would be going together as a couple? Had he issued the invitation as a friend?

In her right hand, she held a blue dress that was sweet and friendly—white collar, nipped-in waist. She always wore it with a string of her grandmother's pearls.

In her left hand, she held a black dress she had never worn. She'd bought it because it was black, but when she'd tried it on, it didn't qualify as a mourning garment. Too short, too tight, a little sexy black lace across the bodice that hinted of…

"Hey, Maria? Are you up there?" Amy Carlson called from the stairs.

"Come on up," Maria called.

"Way too many stairs," Amy told her, huffing into the bedroom. She sat on the bed. "Where's the shrimp?"

"He's at my mother's house for the weekend," Maria explained as she stood in front of the full-length mirror, holding the dresses.

"What are you doing?" Amy asked.

"Trying to decide what to wear," Maria answered.

"Where are you going?"

"To the dance." Maria turned to her. "What do you think?"

"I think it's wonderful!" Amy jumped up and hugged her tightly. "After all this time! It's Sheriff Hunk, isn't it?"

Maria grinned. Then frowned. "I think so. I think he asked me to go with him last night."

"And you're trying to decide what to wear." Amy stated the obvious. "Did he ask you to go with him or go *with* him?"

Laughing, Maria sat beside her on the blue and green comforter. "That's what I've been asking myself."

"Have you kissed him?"

Maria nodded, and both of them laughed.

"Well," Amy demanded, "how was it?"

"It was—" she cleared her throat "—it was pretty good."

"Pretty good?"

"All right," Maria admitted with a slow smile. "It was awesome."

They looked at the dresses again. "Awesome, huh?" Amy said. "Definitely the black. I have a pair of heels that will go with it. And what are you going to do with your hair?"

They piled it loosely on her head, letting a few strands curl down her neck.

"In that dress," Amy assured her, "with my heels and your legs, nobody will be looking at your hair. But I think this'll look great. I have some Rum Raisin lipstick in the car."

"Thanks, Amy." Maria hugged her. "I'm a little nervous."

"Oh, Maria! This is exactly what you've needed to do. Get out, kiss gorgeous men! Josh would've wanted you to go on. He would've wanted you to live."

Maria didn't have time to dwell on her words. As Amy went to her car, the phone rang.

"How's that foot today?"

"It's fine. Not even sore," she replied.

"So, I can expect at least one dance?" he asked.

"I haven't danced in years," she confessed, looking at herself in the mirror as she spoke. A wide smile was stretched across her face.

"Then I think it must be time," he said reassuringly. "I'll pick you up at eight, if that works for you?"

"Eight is fine," she answered, nodding. Her hair fell back down her back. "By then I should be ready."

He laughed and said something else before he hung up. Maria missed his last words, thinking, instead, how much she liked his laugh.

"That was him, wasn't it?" Amy asked, breathless from her run up the stairs.

"That was him," Maria confirmed. "Oh, God! It's like being seventeen again."

"You're lucky," Amy replied, handing her friend the tube of lipstick. "I'm going with Steve Landis."

"Steve?" Maria choked out his name. "He's, well, he's nice."

Amy shrugged. "Never mind. He keeps his car really clean, anyway. I think we need a bigger clip for your hair."

They put makeup on each other and did each other's hair. Maria tried on her dress, and Amy analyzed her friend critically.

"You look like you're trying to hide something,"

she said, finishing a piece of lemon pound cake and brushing the crumbs from her hands.

"It's just so darn short." Maria urged the dress down another inch, but the material wouldn't comply.

"It looks fantastic," Amy said. "Just hold your shoulders back and let them all die of envy."

Maria considered her friend's words as she stood inside the doorway waiting for Joe that night. She had brushed her hair until her head ached, ruined three pairs of black panty hose and dropped her lipstick in the toilet.

Her hands were shaking, and she could feel her skirt riding higher. She made a decision to change and would have run up the stairs, but headlights flashed in her driveway.

Joe was here. She would have to go, despite her mixed feelings about her appearance. She pulled on her coat, careful of her hair, and walked out before she could change her mind.

The night was cold but the truck was warm inside, pleasantly scented with his aftershave. She looked at him in the dim light, and her heart did a little dance.

"Hi," he greeted her. "I would've come up—"

"Oh, there's no reason," she insisted, trying to sound more prosaic than she felt. "I think we know each other well enough. I mean, we work together now. There's no reason to make a fuss."

"Where's Sam tonight?" he asked, backing the truck out of the driveway.

"He's with my mother for the weekend," she answered then wished she had bitten her tongue. Nothing like making herself sound available. The man would be running in terror before the night was over.

Joe glanced her way. She sounded strange. "He told me he was going to do some fishing."

"He loves fishing almost as much as he loves computers."

Was she having second thoughts? he wondered, listening to the faint tremor in her voice. Was she sorry she'd agreed to go out with him?

He had done some soul searching. He was dressed and ready an hour early. Thinking about Rachel and Maria. Feeling guilty and nervous on one hand and just plain nervous on the other.

"So this dance is a pretty big affair," he observed as they approached the main street of Gold Springs.

"It's been going on for almost a hundred years," she replied, glad of the familiar topic. "The old saloon is maintained just for tonight. The dance begins Founder's Week for the town, ending in Founder's Day for the tourists."

"I've heard that Dennie Lambert's punch is something to watch out for."

She laughed. "That's true. I remember when I was a little girl and my mother would be getting ready to go to the Founder's Dance. It was the equivalent of Cinderella's ball around here. She used to remind my dad not to drink too much punch and make a fool of himself."

They reached the center of the old town, and he parked the truck in the crowded parking area, then turned off the ignition. "Did he pay attention?"

"I don't know." She thought about it. "I never saw them come home. It was always too late."

"Why aren't they coming this year?" he asked, hating to leave the truck and enter the crowded building. He would prefer to have her all to himself.

"My father died when I was still in school," she explained, hoping she didn't sound maudlin. "My mother prefers to stay home and watch game shows and gossip on the phone."

"My parents died when my sister and I were young, too," he responded quietly. "For a long time, it was only the two of us. Then she grew up and got married. She's got a good life."

"But sometimes you wish they hadn't all left you so soon?" she guessed.

He nodded. "Sometimes…but not tonight. Tonight, we're going to Cinderella's ball."

"I'm afraid I'm more likely to be one of the stepsisters than Cinderella," Maria told him ruefully.

He touched her cheek with a warm finger. "That's just as well. I'm not Prince Charming, and I heard that Cinderella is going to end up with him."

She drew a deep breath, wishing she could see his eyes in the darkness. "I guess we might as well make our entrance. I might not be Cinderella, but I haven't been out in such a long time, I might still turn into a pumpkin at midnight."

Joe laughed and came around to help her from the truck. "I don't want you falling in any mine shafts," he told her, opening the door. "How's your knee?"

She turned, and both legs in their black stockings were exhibited for his gaze in the dim light from the saloon.

"It's fine," she managed to say as he carefully perused her legs.

"I'll have to agree with that statement," he said with a smile in his voice. "And the other one seems to be in great shape, too."

"I, uh—"

She slid from the truck seat and into his arms, and he caught her against his chest.

"Second thoughts, Maria?" he whispered in her ear.

"Third and fourth," she answered huskily, but her mouth was ready for him when his lips found hers.

Music filtered out from the gala event inside the century-old building. A cool breeze flirted with the silky hem of her dress and caressed her cheek.

When she was in his arms, everything was all right. The world spun crazily, but it was the right axis for her. Her lips were made for his kisses.

"Don't worry so much," he whispered then kissed her neck.

"I worry about things as a hobby," she replied softly as she touched his face. "What are you doing in my life?"

His kiss fell on her forehead and the curve of her lips. He looked at her with a hunger in his eyes that was unmistakable. "The same thing you're doing in mine."

He drew her closer, and she didn't resist. His warmth and his well-muscled body made her shiver and press closer to him. His kisses drew the strength from her but filled her with wonder.

In all the years she'd loved Josh, she had never felt that heady exhilaration. The emotions that surged through her at Joe's touch were deeper, stronger than any she had ever felt for her young husband.

And that thought made her suddenly feel the bite of the wind. The ghost of treachery trickled its icy finger of guilt down her spine.

"We should go in," she said soberly, drawing away from him. It was the last place she wanted to be, but her thoughts were too painful to face in his arms.

"You're right," he said in a voice he hardly recognized as his own. He wanted to ask her to stay there with him, to drive back to her house and forget the town and its petty squabbles. He wanted to make love to her and lay the ghost of her husband to rest.

He wanted too much, he realized as he felt her withdrawal. He drew a deep breath and held her close for an instant longer, inhaling the fragrance that was her, wishing vainly that he had met her first, that Sam had been his child.

Wishing his own past had been different and that the shadows weren't constantly catching up to him. How could he ask another woman to share his life when he knew it was a mistake?

How could he ask this woman to risk everything for him?

"I—I wish—" She tried and failed to find words for what she wanted.

"I know," he said, then moved purposely away from her. "I wish it, too."

"But you don't know what it is," she reminded him, the light catching the smile she couldn't hold back when she looked at him.

He took her hand and started to walk toward the saloon before he forgot his vow of patience. "Whatever it is," he said magnanimously, "I don't mind adding my wishing power to it."

"Even if it was something you wouldn't like?" she asked.

He looked at her, his hand poised on the door handle. "If it would make you happy, Maria, count me in."

She looked back at him, his light touch on her hand making a warmth spread up her arm. Thoughts and feelings ached to be released. She opened her lips to speak when the doors were flung open, and the light and noise from inside the old-time saloon spilled into the street.

"Sheriff! Maria! Don't stand out there in the cold!"

They would have been separated by the crowd if Joe hadn't kept a loose but purposeful grip on her hand. She felt eyes on her, some questioning, some jealous. Some angry.

A hostess dressed in red satin and a feather boa took her coat. E.J. Marks, with a fake handlebar mustache and a black and white striped shirt, was serving sarsaparilla in mason jars.

The band kicked off another tune, and the laughter and talking roared across her thoughts. Joe turned from the group that had gathered around them when they entered the saloon, and his voice was drowned out as he asked her to dance.

Maria knew what he wanted without hearing the words. She followed his lead and turned into his arms when they reached the dance floor. She pretended to look around them, afraid that if she looked into his dark eyes he would see the love and conflict she felt inside of her.

"It's really loud in here," he said near her ear.

"That's part of Founder's Day," she responded.

"The whole town must be out tonight."

Maria nodded, catching sight of the Lightner clan, minus Tommy, standing to one side of the bandstand. Ricky watched them mutinously, his face still scratched and bruised in places.

The look on Anna Lightner's face could only be described as malevolent. Her eyes followed them, glittering with anger.

"The whole town is watching the new sheriff," she

reminded him, smoothing a hand down the front of his pristine white shirt. It felt new to her fingers, just out of the package.

His black coat and trousers were sharply creased, and his tie was carefully conservative. She knew she'd always like him best in his jeans, though the sheriff's uniform...

He looked at her, catching her eyes with his devilish gaze. "I thought they were all looking at that dress."

Maria felt hot color flood her face. "I know it's a little—" she twitched the skirt "—short."

Joe's eyes followed the movement. The black skirt flirted higher on her shapely thigh. A shaft of pure desire stabbed deeply, making him want to groan. "Maria, please, don't try to make it better. Leave me some dignity."

"I should have worn something—"

"Less tempting?" he suggested.

"Something long and loose and mothering," she said with an angry glance at Amy, who drifted by in Steve's arms.

Amy's dress was purely romantic. Midnight blue lace covered black taffeta falling in folds to the floor. Her blond hair was piled loosely, and her blue eyes had a dreamy look.

Joe spun Maria into a fast turn as the tempo of the music changed and the dance became a two-step. "I like the combination," he remarked. "Angel-blue eyes and bad-girl dress. It makes me wonder which one is the real you."

Maria was saved from replying by the fast music. She was certainly no temptress, but when he looked at her with that sexy light in his eyes, it did make her think of things that were hardly safe or mothering.

"I think I should sit this one out," she told him breathlessly when the music finally stopped. Her foot was sore. The crowd around them clapped enthusiastically.

"I could use some more sarsaparilla," he agreed, taking her arm. They made their way through the crowd to the chairs against the wall.

While Joe went for the drinks, Maria hazarded a look at the Lightners, noticing that Tommy had joined them. He smiled at her and nodded, then bent to whisper something into Ricky's ear. He slapped Ricky on the back as they both broke out into laughter.

There was something going on. She could feel it. The Lightners didn't forgive and forget, at least not in their lifetimes. All she could do was wait for the boom to explode. Josh always said his family was like a powder keg waiting for someone to light the fuse.

Maria glanced around the room nervously, wondering if she should warn Joe. What would she say? For the most part, Gold Springs seemed to like and accept him. But it would take a miracle for the Lightners to let him stay in town.

But she knew Joe wouldn't be moved off that easily. He was as stubborn and single-minded as the Lightners. Joe Roberts could match them any day.

"Miss me?" The object of her thoughts spoke as he returned with jars full of red liquid.

She sipped from her glass and watched him sit beside her. "How do I answer that question?" she teased. "If I say yes, you'll think I can't live without you. If I say no, you'll think I don't care."

He smiled and touched a curl near her ear. "Life is full of tough choices."

"All right then." She paused for effect, leaning closer to him. "Yes, I missed you."

He looked around, as though there might be someone listening, then leaned closer so their heads were nearly touching. "Does that mean you can't live without me?"

She looked at his mouth, and her own went suddenly dry. His dark eyes were filled with the real question behind the flirty game.

"I don't think I'd like to try," she answered bravely, her gaze intent.

Beyond words, his dark head bent closer to hers until there was no music, no lights. No other people around them. Maria felt her eyes flutter closed of their own volition and her lips parted.

"Hell of a night for a dance, eh, Sheriff?" A voice startled her, and she and Joe drew sharply apart.

"Hell of a dance, Billy," Joe drawled, his voice not quite steady.

"Sheriff." Dennie and Mandy Lambert approached simultaneously. The costumes they wore every year glittered garishly in the light. "We've been waiting for our dances."

"Go on," Billy encouraged him. "I'll keep Maria company."

"Me, first," Dennie whined.

"You're always first," Mandy retorted.

"Sheriff, you'll just have to choose," Dennie decided, preening in her green satin gown. A huge ostrich feather appeared to be growing out of the middle of her head.

Joe looked at Maria apologetically then did his duty by the town's oldest residents.

"Dances pretty good," Billy observed, watching

Mandy and her prize shuffle across the old wooden dance floor.

"Looks pretty good, too." Amy joined them with Steve in tow.

Steve Landis took a seat. "Hi, Maria. Things are pretty tight with the sheriff and you, huh?"

"Things are private, Steve," Amy cautioned him bluntly with a warning frown.

"Not so private," Billy added. "Everyone in town has seen them looking moony-eyed at each other."

Amy shrugged, admitting silently that it was true. "You look great in that dress," she told Maria with a secret smile.

"Yeah," Steve said, "you look better than I've ever seen you look."

His eyes were glued to the long length of leg the dress left uncovered. Maria started to pull at the hem but thought better of it after recalling Joe's comment. She held her shoulders back and sipped her punch with what she hoped looked like uncaring nonchalance.

The night wore on, and the music got louder. Maria danced with Steve and with Billy. She saw Joe dancing with Amy then with Ruby Taylor, a waitress from the café who had aspirations to be a dancer in Las Vegas. Tammy Marlowe took a turn with him and left her fake beauty mark on his cheek when she kissed him.

By nine, Maria was hard-pressed to decide which hurt the worst, her feet or her head. She sat on a chair and refused to dance with anyone, watching from the sidelines as the dancers whirled by on the floor.

"You're making a fool of yourself, you know," Tommy told her, sitting next to her unexpectedly.

She glanced at him then looked at the dance floor. "You being the expert—"

"You don't need to put yourself any farther on our bad side," he reminded her. "Do you think Josh would like this? He wouldn't want his wife and his son helping some stranger who's trying to take over Gold Springs."

Maria sighed, not wanting to have the conversation but seeing no way out of it. "Joe's not a dictator, Tommy. He's the sheriff. And if we don't like him in two years, we can vote him right out. But I don't think that's going to happen. Neither do you. He's doing a good job, and everyone except for the Lightners knows it."

"He's managed to fool almost everyone. But we know the truth about him."

"What are you talking about, Tommy? Fool us how? By being there when someone needs help? By making sure the law isn't broken even when it's a law that Ricky doesn't like?" she demanded. "I think you better take a look around you."

"Oh, we've gone easy on the sheriff until now," Tommy retorted sharply, sipping something that wasn't sarsaparilla from a mason jar.

"What do you mean?"

He looked at her, his blue eyes bloodshot but laughing. "You'll see, Maria. And then you'll have to decide for yourself what's going to happen. Either you're with us or you're not. Don't forget, you're a Lightner, too."

Maria watched him walk away, wanting to know what he was planning yet not wanting to go into it with him.

She wanted to leave. She'd put in her appearance. It was warm in the saloon, with the old wood heaters going full blast.

She stood to look for Joe across the packed dance

floor and saw him standing in a group that included Mike Matthews, Sue Drake and another county commissioner.

Feeling her eyes on him, he turned his head to look at her. It didn't take a psychic to know she was ready to leave. He'd noticed Tommy Lightner gravitating in her direction and had watched their animated debate.

He excused himself and waded through the crowd in her direction, feeling like a salmon trying to swim upstream.

He reached her as the saloon doors opened and both deputies on patrol hurriedly searched the room for him.

"Sheriff." The first man he'd hired as a deputy reached him, wiping the steam from his glasses with a careless hand.

He was Arliss Tucker, from the *Gold Springs Bugle,* the town's only newspaper. "You'll need to see this."

"What's wrong?" Maria asked.

"I don't know yet," he admitted with a frown. "Let me find someone to give you a ride to your truck."

"I'll be fine," she replied confidently. "See what's wrong. I can find my own way home."

He searched her eyes, knowing it wouldn't be the last time he would have to leave her. Wasn't that part of his reason for being alone? Wasn't that how he'd lost Rachel?

But he had no choice. "All right. I'm sorry, Maria."

E.J. Marks stepped closer to her after the sheriff left.

"What's up?" Maria asked him quietly.

"Somebody trashed the sheriff's office," he explained, tight-lipped. "And that's not all." He handed her a flyer with a woman's picture on it. "They're all over town."

Chapter Nine

Sunday morning dawned bright, clear and cold in Gold Springs. By late Saturday night, everyone knew what had happened at the sheriff's office.

Maria had spoken with several people on the phone, including her mother. Since everyone knew she worked with the sheriff, everyone assumed she knew the whole story.

Joe wasn't one of the people she'd talked with that night. She'd waited up past midnight for him to call or come by, but there was no word from him.

She'd fallen asleep on the sofa with the phone in her hand. She awakened to someone knocking on the door and a stiff neck. The low battery light was flashing on her phone. She hung it up quickly, tightened the sash on her robe and hurried to the door.

"I tried calling but your phone was off the hook," Joe explained, standing big and very real in her doorway. The sunlight streamed across his tired features. "I was worried about you."

"I went to sleep and left the phone off the hook," she answered, noticing that he still wore his dark suit and tie. The white shirt was rumpled under the open jacket. "You look like you could use some coffee."

He smiled, but his eyes were dull. "I think I could use a whole pot."

She held the door open. "I'm just about to put one on. I can put on one for you, too."

"I don't want to put you to any trouble," he replied, even as he walked into the kitchen.

"No problem," she assured him. "I was about to make breakfast, too, if you can stay."

"I'd like that."

Maria tried to decide if she should run upstairs and change, looked at his drawn face and decided not to worry about it. Her hair was off her face, and her old blue robe was clean. That would have to do.

"So, what happened?" she asked as she took down a big skillet.

"Someone walked into the office, destroyed most of the furniture, threw paint all over everything and walked out."

She frowned. "I'd heard it was bad."

"I suppose everyone knows about it already," he mused, taking off his coat.

"Everyone thinks they know," she explained. "That's the way small towns work. Little bits of gossip pass between people. Hardly anyone ever knows the whole story."

"There was some graffiti, too. Basically, the whole thing was designed to make me look incompetent."

"How so?" she asked, measuring coffee into the machine.

He yawned and shrugged. "I've seen it before. If

you can make people think a sheriff can't take care of his own property, how can he protect yours?''

''I'm sure no one will think that,'' she said, taking out eggs and bread. ''Do you have any idea who did it?''

''Do you?'' he countered baldly.

She looked across a cabinet at him. ''Do you mean you think I'm part of this effort?''

He stared at her without flinching. ''That's not what I meant, Maria.''

''Then what did you mean, Sheriff?'' she demanded.

He sighed and ran a hand through his hair. ''People who have lived in a place for a long time notice things that strangers don't notice. That's why community crime watch groups work so well. Have you noticed anything out of the ordinary? Have you heard anything on the town's grapevine about this?''

Maria's thoughts darted at once to the dance. Tommy Lightner hadn't been at the dance when they'd arrived, and he'd hinted that things were going to be unpleasant for the sheriff. Could he have been responsible for the damage?

''I can't think of anything,'' she lied, wondering at her sense of right and wrong. She couldn't bring herself to tell Joe what she suspected. She didn't have the right to implicate Tommy when he might be innocent.

Joe watched her face as she set a mug of coffee in front of him. If her face had been blank, he would have felt better. Maria Lightner was a bad liar.

''I did notice that Tommy Lightner wasn't at the dance last night until after eight-thirty.'' He tried to make it easier for her.

She glanced at him sharply. ''That doesn't make him a criminal.''

"Of course not," he agreed. "It could make him a suspect. He and his family have made their feelings clear about me."

Maria cracked eggs into the frying pan with a trembling hand. Part of her agreed with him but another part of her refused to believe that Tommy would stoop so low. He was family, after all, despite everything. He was Josh's brother, and he'd wanted to be sheriff himself.

"Talking about how you feel doesn't make you a criminal, either," she replied coolly.

"What was he talking to you about last night?" Joe asked, despite the warning flags of color in her face. "Your conversation looked pretty angry."

Maria flipped the eggs in the pan and pushed the lever down on the toaster. "Are you asking me this as the sheriff and as part of your investigation? Or as Joe Roberts, interested friend?"

They stared at each other across the stove. Maria finally looked away to flip the eggs from the pan to two plates.

"I'll get the toast," he offered, coming around the counter.

They sat across the wooden table from each other. Maria scooted her eggs around her plate with her fork while Joe sipped his coffee. The noisy ticking of her grandmother's wooden cuckoo clock filled the silence between them.

"I'm both," he finally answered. "I don't know if I can be one without the other."

Maria stabbed her egg with her fork, and the yellow center filled her plate. "Then I don't know if I can answer that question."

"Are you telling me that after all the work you've

done trying to get the office ready to open, you think it was okay for Tommy Lightner to waltz in there and trash the building?''

She looked at him. His dark eyes held an angry fire.

''I'm telling you that I don't know if Tommy did this. I wasn't there. Neither were you.''

''No,'' he agreed, heatedly. ''I was conveniently out with you.''

Maria stood up slowly, all the color draining from her face. ''I'm going up to get dressed. You can let yourself out when you're finished.''

''Maria, I—''

She slammed the kitchen door behind her. Joe ran a hand across his eyes, knowing he needed some sleep. Knowing his words had been hasty and unwarranted. Of course he didn't believe Maria had led him around while Tommy Lightner sneaked up behind him.

Of course he'd been a fool. He was a tired fool with more to lose than just a job. Gold Springs had become more than a step in his career. He wanted a life here. He wanted the people to respect him and he wanted to make them feel safe.

He wanted Maria. But he needed some sleep and a shower, and she needed some time to cool off before he tried to explain. He hoped he could find the words to apologize and make her understand, but at the moment, his brain was beyond thought.

He put their plates and cups in her dishwasher. Then he saw the poster. It was shoved into a corner on her counter.

He held it in his hands, and all the old memories flooded his senses. It was Rachel, of course. The picture was a bad one. It didn't show the fire in her eyes or the sunlight in her hair. He looked at her beautiful face and heard her laughter and her tears.

No doubt the Lightners looked at her and saw the one blemish on his record as a way of making him lose trust with the people of Gold Springs.

He looked up the stairs, thinking about trying to explain to Maria. Wondering why she hadn't asked him about the grainy newspaper picture and its inflammatory caption.

"Rachel Andrews, twenty-three, lost her life in a fatal car crash that had been attributed to alcohol. U.S. Marshal Joseph Roberts has been suspended as his part in yesterday's wreck on the city's south side is explored. Miss Andrews was Sheriff Roberts's fiancé. Do we want a man responsible for a drunken car wreck as the sheriff for our town?"

He crumpled the paper slowly and locked the door behind him when he left her house.

His truck was still in her driveway when he realized something was wrong. Both patrol cars and three fire trucks were in the road and lining his driveway.

Walking up from the street, he noticed the heavy smoke and the acrid smell of fire. He knew before he reached the clearing that everything was gone. Several loads of lumber he'd had delivered the week before along with the lumber he'd saved from taking down the Hannon house was burned.

"Sheriff." Arliss Tucker, notebook in hand, nodded to him.

"Lightning strike?" Joe mused tiredly.

"Could be." Arliss looked him squarely in the eye. "In a manner of speaking."

"Everything's destroyed," the fire chief told him bluntly. "If you had insurance—"

"Did it look accidental?" Joe asked.

The fire chief shook his head. "I'd bet gasoline, my-self. Poured over everything and lit up. It was fast and hot, Sheriff. Sorry."

"There wasn't much, anyway," Joe told him dispir-itedly.

"We'll be investigating," the chief assured him. "This is arson, whether it was a scare tactic or not. The law is the law."

Joe shook his hand. "Thanks."

"I'm afraid they even got the electric pole, Sheriff," Arliss told him with a shake of his graying head.

Joe knew he was tired when he had the incredible urge to laugh. "I guess I'll have to find another one."

The fire chief glanced at Arliss. Both men had the grace to look ashamed.

"I'd like to help," Arliss said. "We have a spare room in our house. It's not much, but—"

"Thanks, but I have a place in mind," Joe answered with a tight smile.

Understanding dawned in Arliss's eyes, and he nod-ded. "Sure. I didn't think. Well, anyway. Anything I can do, Sheriff."

The fire chief reiterated the words, and the three men shook hands, then the trucks went to the fire station. Arliss drove in to make the evening edition of the *Bugle*. The two deputies wandered around the scene until Joe told them to resume their patrols.

"Keep your eyes open," he warned them. "This might not be the end of it."

The two men were shaken but committed. They got into their patrol cars and left him standing in the ashes of what might have been his home.

Not one of them asked about the poster, but he could feel the question in their eyes.

Were you responsible?

Hadn't the Internal Affairs people asked him that question a dozen times before they were satisfied? Hadn't he asked himself that question every day since that terrible night?

Joe looked at the mess through bleary eyes. His mind refused to function. He couldn't acknowledge the loss or make decisions. He parked his truck in the driveway then climbed into the camper and went to sleep.

Maria spent the afternoon going over her accounts, trying to find the money to pay off loans for the truck and the furnace. Without ever seeing Joe Roberts again.

She had been angry at first. Angry that he would accuse her of playing up to him as part of some plot, angry that he didn't trust her. Angry that she wondered about the woman on the poster.

Rachel Andrews. *Had* Joe been responsible for her death? Hadn't Maria felt more than once that Joe knew what it was to deal with loss?

She knew, without a doubt, that this woman had been the information the Lightners had found to use against the sheriff. They'd hinted at it, but she'd ignored them, thinking Joe could take care of himself.

Now, she wasn't so sure.

Once she'd dressed and cleaned the house, she felt empty. The passion of anger would have been a relief in the face of the terrible blankness that threatened to engulf her. Before she'd met Joe, her life had been placid. Sometimes lonely, but she'd tried not to let it defeat her.

After realizing she had allowed herself to fall in love with him, she was filled with the emptiness his leaving would mean to her. She had only begun to think her future might not be so bleak. There had been a bright ray of promise in Joe's dark eyes that had called her heart into the sunlight.

She tried to pull herself together as she drove to pick up Sam. Her mother lived just outside of town. It wouldn't be enough time to clear her face if she started to cry. It wouldn't do to have to explain red puffy eyes to her mother.

A hundred phone calls had probably described what she'd been wearing the night before and how she'd danced with Joe. She didn't want to talk about the turn their relationship had taken. Or Rachel Andrews.

Could he really believe she had been helping Tommy? Maria wondered in spite of herself. The town had given him a hard time, and she had acknowledged she'd known about the Hannon house. In a perverse way, she was flattered. As far as she knew, no one had ever considered her hypnotically· beautiful. By admitting his attention was so tightly fixed on her that he didn't pay attention to his job, Joe was giving his feelings away.

Not that he'd made those feelings a secret, she thought, a smile starting despite her best efforts to squash it.

The way he'd kissed her. She hadn't known there was a place where there was no room for thought or fear. When she was in his arms, she was flying, as light and as free as any bird.

True, she had paid for those feelings with a bout of guilt, but something Amy had said made sense to her. Josh had never been a selfish man. He wouldn't have wanted her to stay at home and never live in the world again. He wouldn't have wanted her to cry for him when she looked at their son.

What she felt for Joe was stronger, more awe-inspiring. Maybe she was just older, and the loss of her husband at such a young age had sharpened her senses.

She didn't believe she loved Joe any more than she had Josh. It was the love of an older woman. A woman who had grieved and gone on with life, never guessing that something so remarkable could still be in store for her.

Yet, there were still questions to be answered. What if Joe believed she had a part in destroying the sheriff's office? What if he left Gold Springs blaming her for betraying him?

What if he couldn't answer the questions that were sure to come about the woman in the poster?

Uncle Pete and Sam were coming up from the creek when she pulled into the yard. Maria knew she would have to put her questions to the side and cope with her mother and her son. There was nothing to do but ask Joe if he was serious about his accusations. She could only hope he wasn't.

"The fish weren't biting," Sam told her, holding up a long, empty string.

"We're gonna eat all that other good food your mama's been gettin' ready for lunch if you want to stay, Maria," Uncle Pete invited with his open smile.

"I'd like that," she returned, hugging him. "Is Mom in the house?"

"Where else?" he asked. "Can't get her off that damn phone. Night and day. Somebody did this to somebody else. Makes me wish I had just gone on with your father."

Maria frowned. "You could move out on your own," she told her mother's brother.

"And wash my own clothes?" he demanded with a laugh. "C'mon, Sam. Let's put this stuff away. We'll try again next week."

"I guess I'll go in," Maria said, staring at the neat white door.

"You might as well. You've been the topic of conversation all morning. I heard that was some dress you wore last night."

"It was a little short," she admitted with a grin.

"And a little tight," he added. "And I heard that sheriff's eyes almost popped out of his head when he saw it."

"Joe likes her a lot." Sam volunteered the comment with a toothy grin.

"Never mind," Maria answered, shooing them away. "I'm going in to take my medicine."

Her mother was on the phone in the spotless green and yellow kitchen, but the minute her daughter walked through the door, she hung up.

"Well, that was quite a night last night," her mother observed.

"Good morning, Mom," Maria replied, kissing her mother's pink cheek.

"What dress did you wear, honey? I don't think I've ever seen a creation like the one I've been hearing described."

"It was a dress I bought years ago, but it was too short and too tight," Maria told her. It wouldn't do any good to lie about it. She'd find out anyway.

Barbara Auden nodded. "That's as I thought." She filled a pot with water and set it on the stove. "So what about the sheriff, Maria? I've been hearing all week about the two of you. That he paid to get your furnace fixed and the two of you went to the Founder's Dance after you haven't gone since Josh's death. Sam has talked nonstop about him.''

Maria shook her head. ''I think you already know everything, Mom. You might be able to tell me a thing or two.''

Her mother looked at her slyly as she started to get lunch together. ''I suppose you already know about the fire.''

''Fire?'' Maria asked, startled.

''I heard from Mandy Lambert a few minutes ago. It might have happened as you were driving out here,'' her mother said, pleased that she knew something her daughter didn't know. ''Someone burned the sheriff's house, such as it was, and a bunch of new lumber in his yard. The fire chief said it was arson. Someone poured gasoline on all of it and lit a match.''

''Is he all right?'' Maria demanded.

''He wasn't there until it was all over. Someone said they saw his truck in your driveway bright and early this morning.''

The two women faced each other in the cheerful kitchen. Maria had her father's coloring, but she was a perfect model for her mother's classic good looks.

There the resemblance ended. Maria was more like her father than her mother in personality. Barbara Auden despaired of her only daughter's life. She had wanted so much for the girl. Her father had only wanted her to be happy.

''He came to tell me about the office,'' Maria explained. ''He knew I'd be interested since I've been working there with him.''

''Looks pretty bad for Tommy and Ricky, doesn't

it?'' her mother interjected with the art of an expert meddler. "He does suspect them, doesn't he?"

"I don't know," Maria lied, not wanting to get into that conversation. "He's the sheriff, but the county will probably send in an arson investigator."

Barbara sighed. "Everyone noticed Tommy was late getting to the dance. It doesn't take a genius to put that together. You did say the sheriff wasn't a moron, didn't you?"

Maria laughed. "He's tall, dark and handsome, Mom. As I'm sure you know. He's smart and funny and he likes Sam. He takes his job too seriously, though, and I'm afraid if I do get involved with him, I might lose him. He's a hero. Just like Josh."

Barbara's expressive face grew serious as she sat opposite her daughter at the kitchen table. "Just because it happened once doesn't mean it would happen again, honey. If you think this could work for you, grab it. There aren't many second chances for happiness."

Maria was astounded. "He's nobody, Mom. Not a Lightner or a Lambert."

Her mother sniffed self-righteously. "He's the sheriff. People like him and respect him already. In ten years' time, no one will even recall that he wasn't born here."

"And it wouldn't hurt you to be related to the sheriff," Maria guessed.

Barbara took her hand and stared into her daughter's blue eyes with uncharacteristic sadness. "I know what it is to lose someone you love. But your father and I had a lot of good years together. You deserve that, too, Maria. You and Sam both deserve to have someone in your lives."

For a minute, she glimpsed a part of her mother she

hadn't known existed. Was there something besides her machinations and gossip that Maria had missed all those years?

It was gone in the next blink of an eyelid. Uncle Pete and Sam came in with growling stomachs and dirty hands. Sam's chattering covered up the awkward silence that lingered after her mother's words.

Maria shook her head, dazed, not really sure it had happened. Whatever had spurred her mother into those insightful words was hidden behind a veil of silver blue eyeshadow and a bright green apron.

They ate lunch in a festive mood, talking about Founder's Day.

"I heard the sheriff is going to dedicate the new mine shaft they found last spring," Barbara told them all as she served banana pudding. "I hope he has his speech prepared."

Maria hoped so, too, but she didn't say so. Joe hadn't said anything to her about a speech, but she wouldn't put it past the Lambert sisters, who ran Founder's Day, to ask him.

"That's the shaft they say that boy was killed in," Uncle Pete observed, sitting back. "Right after the war. That's why it was closed up and people forgot about it."

"Just another ghost story." Barbara dismissed his words.

"Maybe so." Uncle Pete looked into Sam's bright eyes. "But I wouldn't want to be there after dark."

Sam pestered him for the story, but Maria told him it was time to go.

"We'll tell it during the week," Uncle Pete promised with a smile at the boy. "Have a good time at school."

"Are you going to marry Joe?" Sam asked after they'd left his grandmother's house.

Maria took her eyes off the road for an instant. "Did someone tell you that, Sam?"

"Not really," he admitted with a shrug. "I was thinking about it."

"We don't know each other well enough," she explained. "You have to know someone a while before you marry them."

"How long?" Sam wondered. "How long did you know Dad?"

Maria smiled. "We grew up together. When I was ten, he painted my face orange on Halloween. It wouldn't come off with soap and water, and I had to go to school every day for two weeks before it finally wore away."

Sam laughed. "But you loved him later."

"I did, Sam. I loved him a lot."

"You wouldn't have to forget him to marry Joe, would you? I mean, we could still talk about him and stuff."

"If I marry Joe," she promised, "we'll still talk about him. He'll still be your dad, no matter what. Joe could never take his place."

"But Joe makes you smile," Sam said with all the knowing of an eight-year-old. "I think he likes me, too."

"I think he does," Maria agreed. "But let's not rush things, okay? Let's know each other for a while longer before we think about anything else."

"Okay," Sam replied and moved on to other topics.

They swung by the Hannon place and took a look at the scorched earth and what was left of the house.

Joe's truck was gone, and a call to the office was answered by a deputy who had no idea where the sheriff was.

Maria sent Sam off to school the next morning and took her courage in hand, dressed, and went into the office. If Joe was serious about the things he'd said to her, he would have had time to think about it. It was as well to find out. She knew she would have a lifetime to mourn his loss in her life.

The office was locked up tight when she parked her truck in the lot, but a large group of people met her at the door.

"We're here about what happened," the carpenter said. His entire crew was there. "And to repair the hole in the floor."

Mandy Lambert led another group who wanted to help clean up the mess. Painters and electricians paraded into the office, all wanting to help put it into shape.

It was worse than Maria had thought. Paint had been smeared everywhere from ceiling to floor, all over papers and files, across toilets and lights. Every piece of furniture was damaged. Some things could be salvaged. Some were tossed out on a truck to haul to the landfill.

The posters were on every wall, littering the sidewalks outside and the floor inside.

"Such trash!" Mandy dropped one on the floor.

Maria looked at it. Rachel's face was young and pretty despite the graininess of the photo.

"Think he killed that girl?" one of the electricians asked as he nodded at the picture in her hand.

"He'll tell us the truth," Mandy said, taking the poster from Maria and crumpling it into the trash. "Get to work!"

Would he tell them the truth? Maria wondered. Joe seemed to be a very private man despite his very public job. He hadn't confided in her about Rachel or his past. Would he try to explain or would he simply move on to another job?

Doug Ruggles came by and picked up the pieces of the sign he'd worked on, shook his head and promised to do another. The paint on the outside of the old building was whitewashed over by lunchtime, and the sidewalk was being steam cleaned by a crew from Rockford.

Maria bustled around the office, her ears primed for the sound of Joe's voice as everyone worked, but the day passed without him stopping by.

"The sheriff hasn't checked in with the office," she told E.J. Marks when he came in for patrol duty.

"He's gone for the next two days. County commission thing," he explained briefly, with a nervous glance at her.

Maria was quick to read his thoughts. Everyone knew they had been a couple at the dance, and since she didn't know where he was for the next two days, it could only mean one thing. They were no longer a couple.

She didn't enlighten him. She wasn't sure herself what their standing was after Sunday morning. Putting on a smile and a determined air, she supervised the restoration of the office as though her life depended on it.

Mandy Lambert approached her at the end of the long day.

"I think I'm going to call it a day, dear. What a mess! If I get my hands on whoever's responsible…"

"I'm sure when the sheriff gets back he'll want to thank you for all you've done today," Maria told her.

Mandy Lambert did a double take, as did her friend Tammy Marlowe.

"He might want to thank me tonight, Maria," she said gently. "He's staying in my guest room until we can do something about finding him a decent place to live."

Tammy Marlowe patted Maria's arm and smiled mistily. "It'll all work out in the end, Maria."

Maria was sure the two older women went home with a buzz of gossip to spread to their telephone calling circle. Maria learned Mandy Lambert had found the sheriff sleeping in his truck and offered him a place to stay.

Maria jumped at each phone call that night, waiting for the machine to pick up before she answered. She would have answered if it had been Joe, she told herself. Despite her misgivings about talking over the situation on the telephone.

She didn't get the chance, however. There was no word from Joe that night or the next day, while she sorted through papers in the files, trying to save what she could of the records. The office hummed with activity, and the building was beginning to show the signs of progress.

Amy came by and donated two hours to the cause, spending most of the time pumping Maria for information about her breakup with Joe.

"If you let him go," Amy promised with a warning eye, "you'll be sorry the rest of your life. I saw the two of you together. You looked good, really good."

"If he believes I kept him busy while someone did

all this,'' Maria told her wearily, ''I don't see how I can convince him any differently.''

''You might be right,'' Amy replied with an elegant shrug. ''I guess I'll have to snap him up, then.''

''You!''

''Do you want someone else to have him?'' Amy demanded. ''Now that everyone knows he's not with you, Ruby Taylor's going to be all over him.''

''I can't believe she cared whether he was with me or not,'' Maria argued angrily.

''She didn't!'' Amy informed her. ''She's been all over him every morning he's eaten at the café. All but sitting in his lap—''

''Thanks for telling me,'' Maria replied, turning to her files.

''You know I'm only joking,'' Amy said with a laugh. ''But I'm serious about you and Joe. Don't let him get away, Maria.''

Maria sighed. ''If I can help it, I won't.''

Amy checked her watch. ''All right. I have to get back to the real world. The chairman of the street decorating committee can only be inside during lunch. I'll see you later. Call me if you hear anything.''

Out on the street, Gold Springs was being transformed as it was once every year. The tree-lined streets were swept clean and lined with banners and no parking signs. The old buildings, open only one week a year, got their annual coats of paint. Gas streetlights were being primed.

Every year, a few thousand visitors came to the Founder's Day celebration. There were parades and barbecues, storytelling and crafts, as well as tours of the old mining town and shaft sites.

Maria knew with all the work the people of Gold

Springs had put, albeit belatedly, into the new sheriff's office, it would be ready for the festival. For the first time in over fifty years, the city hall would be alive and welcoming visitors into its century-old halls.

Nothing stopped the founder's celebration in Gold Springs, Maria thought. Not bad weather or a new sheriff or a few destructive pranks. Her heart wasn't in it, but everyone had made it clear they knew about it and didn't expect anything any different from her.

Everyone knew she was brokenhearted and that her relationship with Joe was history. Maria bit her lip nervously and waited to find out if it was true.

Chapter Ten

It was Wednesday morning before Joe drove back into Gold Springs. It was the first time he'd seen the town in the daylight since the day of the dance.

Everything had been transformed in the few days he'd been in Rockford. Every building, even the old jail, gleamed with a new coat of paint. Fresh yellow chrysanthemums graced every corner, and wide banners welcomed the crowds. Clowns in colorful suits walked the streets with ladies in bustles holding parasols.

It was strange to feel so connected with a place. He'd only been there a short time, and yet he took great pride in the town and was looking forward to Founder's Day.

And to seeing Maria. The thought of her invoked mixed emotions. He had thought it was wise to let things cool off between them before he apologized, but his work in Rockford had taken longer than he'd planned. He was afraid the cooling-off period might have become a frigid waste.

When he'd come down to breakfast that morning, Mandy Lambert and her sister had started in on him.

"What's happened between you and Maria Lightner is unfortunate, but you shouldn't let it throw you off," Dennie had said prettily.

What had they heard? He didn't dare to ask the wily pair anything. Obviously, Maria had said something about what had happened between them. What had he expected?

He should have called from Rockford. He'd picked up the phone a few times to do just that, but he'd been reluctant to discuss anything with her on the phone.

He knew she'd be in the building working. If she was waiting for the first sight of him to walk out and leave him flat, he couldn't blame her. But he wished she'd hear him out.

Admitting he would never know if he stayed in his truck, as well as noticing the odd looks he was getting from passing acquaintances, he pushed himself out of the vehicle and through the front door of the city hall.

He couldn't believe his eyes. The walls glistened with a new coat of white paint and a chandelier hung from the high ceiling. The crystals sparkled like jewels in the light.

A new reception desk had been placed in the entry, and the woman who sat behind it looked up and smiled as he walked in the door.

"Good morning, Sheriff," she said in a pleasant voice. "I'm Becky Powell. These are your messages, and there's coffee in the kitchen if you'd like a cup."

He nodded, too awed to speak. He'd left the place in chaos and come back to a reality that was even better than before the vandalism.

There were two office doors on the left, one of them

clearly painted "Sheriff." He guessed the other would be Maria's office. He glanced in and saw her head just slightly above the desktop. She was sitting on the floor with her back to the door.

"Hi," he said, leaning against the door frame, content to look at her. The sunlight burned like fire in her hair, and when she turned to look at him, he thought his heart would burst. He wasn't sure how it had happened that he had come to love this woman so completely in such a short time, but there was no denying what he felt for her.

"Hello." She turned to the papers she was going through, neatly laid in stacks on the floor. She couldn't read anything on them after hearing his voice. It was the moment she'd dreaded yet longed for.

"You, uh, the place looks incredible," he told her, trying to find some common ground.

"Everyone's been working hard," she replied without looking at him. "I think it will be ready by Saturday."

He nodded. "That's great. The town has really changed since I left."

"Founder's Day madness," she answered with a smile, her heart pounding. "Nothing is left untouched."

"Maria," he began, fumbling for words.

"Sheriff!" E.J. hailed him from the front door. "Those arson guys from the state are out at your place. They want to talk to you."

Maria glanced at him. "I guess I'll see you later."

"We need to talk," he managed to say before E.J. hurried him from the office. "I'll see you later."

Maria waited the rest of the day, wondering if he had thought the whole thing through and decided he couldn't trust her enough to work here anymore. Wondering if he would explain about Rachel.

Maria left the office that evening without hearing from him. Whatever had gone on out at his place must have been important, she decided as she locked the office door. And time-consuming.

Doug Ruggles's new sign was impressive. He had made the new one even bigger and more elaborate than the sign that had been destroyed.

That's the way Gold Springs had always been, she mused, looking around her at the shadow-filled town. Proud and determined to survive, picking up the pieces time and time again.

She picked Sam up at the Lightners', exchanging stares with Tommy as she waited for her son. She wanted to ask him in plain English if he was responsible for the office being trashed, but she couldn't find the words.

It was probably misguided, but a sense of loyalty kept her silent. They had never been close, but he was Sam's uncle and Josh's brother. They had shared so much grief as a family. She didn't have the heart to ask.

Sam was full of talk about the play, which had suddenly become something he wanted to do. It seemed that one of the angels was a little yellow-haired girl who had winked at him while they were singing.

"She's got braces," he explained, listing her obvious attributes.

"She sounds nice, Sam," Maria replied, knowing it was only the beginning of her son's infatuations. Someday, there would be a girl and they would get married and have children of their own. Someday, she would be a grandmother.

"Look." Sam caught her wandering attention, pointing to their front porch. "There's Joe."

He was right. There was no truck, but Joe was sitting on the stairs. He was dressed in blue jeans and a brown sweater, and when he stood up, the sky blazed behind him with the last dying rays of the sun.

Maria thought she would always remember him that way, no matter what happened between them. He looked tall and lean, and his dark hair was wet, as though he'd just taken a shower. She stared at him hungrily, turning off the truck but not getting out.

"Can he stay for supper?" Sam asked, opening his door.

She nodded. "If he likes—"

"Joe!" Sam hailed him eagerly. "Mom says you can stay for supper."

"Does she?" he asked, not taking his eyes from her face.

"Yeah," Sam assured him, then added confidentially, "and this time, she can cook."

Maria picked up her purse and closed the truck door. She didn't hear his answer and she felt awkward, not knowing what to expect.

"I'd like to talk to your mother alone a minute, Sam," he requested. "If you wouldn't mind."

"No, that's okay," Sam answered quickly. He'd heard the rumors about his mother and the sheriff, listening carefully when he was at his grandparents' house.

"I'll be inside in a minute," Maria promised her son with a vague smile.

"I'm sorry if I'm keeping you."

She reassured him after Sam had closed the door. She didn't have to look up to know her son was watching from the window. "Did you find out anything about the fire?"

He shrugged. "The arson team thinks it was a couple of transients. They picked them up at the scene of another fire out here. They probably did me a favor. The house wasn't worth much, anyway. I guess I'm going to try and sell the land."

She looked at him then. Most of his face was hidden in the shadows. "You're going to let them drive you out of town? I wouldn't have thought you were a quitter."

He smiled at her, wanting nothing so much as to pull her close and kiss her. "I'm going to try to find a place with a house. I don't have time to build right now, but I need a place of my own."

"Oh."

"Would it have mattered?" he asked, wanting to hear her say it.

She folded her arms protectively across her chest. "I think Gold Springs needs you."

He frowned. "Maria, about the other morning, those stupid things I said. I didn't mean any of them. I said them because you and Sam and Gold Springs mean something to me. Something I was afraid of losing." He put his hands on her arms. "I want to tell you about Rachel."

Maria swallowed hard. "The woman in the poster."

They sat on the porch steps, not looking at each other.

"What the poster says is true," he explained, reliving the night fifteen years earlier. "Rachel and I were engaged to be married. She was never happy about me going out and putting my life on the line. She started drinking. I didn't realize, I guess. I was busy, and she seemed all right to me. That night, a friend of mine called me from a bar and told me that I needed to come and pick her up."

He paused, and Maria touched his arm. "You don't have to—"

"It's okay," he said heavily. "What I told you about grieving and letting go? I've been there. Sometimes I'm still there."

Maria was quiet as the evening closed around them.

"I got there and we started arguing. She was crying when I put her in the car. She begged me to quit the force, told me she needed me more than the rest of the world did. I told her my job was important to me. She became hysterical and started hitting me and trying to make me stop the car. She threw herself across the wheel and said she wanted to die."

He looked into the darkening sky. "It was snowing, and roads were icy. I lost control of the car, and it flipped over into a ditch. Rachel was thrown out on the ground and pinned under the car. She died before anyone could reach her."

His voice broke, and Maria hugged her knees tightly, feeling his loss as well as her own.

"They thought I had been drinking too, at first. I was suspended, but there were never any charges filed against me. Eventually, I went back to work, but I knew the truth. I was responsible for her death. I was young and ambitious. I pushed us both to the breaking point. I never saw it until it was too late. She hated me taking risks, risks I saw as necessary to further my career."

He turned to her, taking her hand in his. "When I met you and you told me about Josh, I realized what Rachel must have felt. Josh died a hero, but it didn't matter. He was still gone. I didn't want to hurt Rachel. I don't want to hurt you and Sam.''

Maria moved closer to him until their frosty breaths were mingled in the twilight. "So you decided to live alone rather than hurt someone else or yourself again? That's what I've done, Joe. That's why you and I can't—"

He kissed her swiftly before she could say those awful words. Maria's lips parted, and her sigh met his as their warmth joined them against the night.

"We both have a lot to let go of," he whispered, touching her cheek, which sparkled with a tear. "We both have a long way to go."

Maria blinked, trying to find her voice, Joe's arms around her.

"I'd better go," he said finally, releasing her and standing up. "I wanted you to know the truth and to thank you for all the work you did at the office."

"What about the posters?" she asked, wanting him to stay. "What about your job?"

"I talked with Mike Matthews and some of the county commissioners this morning. Sue Drake knew everything from the beginning," he explained. "They plan on calling a town meeting after Founder's Day. I want it put on the table for everyone."

She sighed. He wasn't leaving. "There might be some questions. But I think everyone is willing to give you a chance, Joe."

He looked at her, wishing he could reach for her. But he could hear the doubt in her voice, and the taste of his own doubt was like ashes in his mouth.

"I think it'll work out, Maria," he agreed. "You've been a big help."

"Thank you," she replied gravely. "I'm so sorry, Joe. About Rachel." *About everything.*

"It was a long time ago," he said in a deep voice then shook his head. "Tomorrow's Founder's Day, right?"

"Rain or shine," she answered, forcing the words through her dry throat.

"I'll see you then."

Maria watched him walk away in the darkness. She wanted to call him back but she couldn't find the words.

"Where's he going, Mom?" Sam's high-pitched voice came through the window.

"He had to take care of a few things," Maria told her son. She wrapped her arms around herself, shivering with the cold and something else.

She was terrified. She thought she'd dealt with her fears about him being the sheriff, but all the old nightmares came rushing back at her.

She could have been Rachel. Joe could have been Josh. Both of them had lost the people they loved because of their beliefs that they could make a difference. That what they did was more important than their lives.

"Are you coming inside, Mom?" Sam asked.

"Yes, Sam," she answered wearily, walking slowly up the steps.

She closed the door on the frozen night, then lay in her bed awake for hours after Sam had gone to sleep, not able to shut out the memories or the warmth of Joe's arms around her.

Founder's Day began bright and early Saturday morning. By eight, there were already crowds of visitors behind the barricades lining the old town streets.

Apple cider stands were set up on every corner manned by familiar faces in unfamiliar, antique clothes.

Music tinkled from the saloon, where shots of sarsaparilla were a dollar apiece, and a group of high school girls danced on the old stage wearing feather boas.

Maria dropped Sam off at the float he had helped decorate and walked quickly through Gold Mine Park in the center of town to reach the parade route.

She watched for Joe, but didn't see him. His deputies were everywhere, but no one else had seen the sheriff, either.

What if he had left town before she had a chance to see him again? What if she had been wrong to let him leave last night before she'd had a chance to think?

She'd had plenty of time to think during the long night. She had forced herself to get up at three and sat watching the morning come glowing through the darkness.

That's what Joe had done to her life, she realized. He'd been a warm glow coming through the cold darkness. A part of her had died with Josh, but another part had come to life when she'd kissed Joe Roberts. She was still terrified of losing him, as she'd lost Josh, but the thought of never seeing him again was devastating.

She finally reached the base of a high mound, part of the excavation of the new shaft. It was quiet here. The park wouldn't officially be open to the public until after the parade and the declaration ceremonies.

In a few weeks, when the project was finished, there would be permanent stairs so tourists could walk to the top of the mine shaft and look through a Plexiglas window at the deep well beneath it.

For the dedication, a temporary platform was set up

over the opening to the shaft. The whole area was draped with red, white and blue tissue paper. A large podium with a microphone was in the middle of the platform.

Maria walked onto the platform, avoiding the podium, hoping to get a better view of the parade and the main street. If Joe was down there, she would be able to see him. If he wasn't... Her heart faltered at the thought.

Where are you, Joe? She glanced around quickly, thinking she'd heard a reply to her unspoken question, but there was no one there. She shivered when she heard another sound and told herself it was the wind. It sounded like someone calling for help.

The sound came again. A voice straining, calling for help.

Maria walked slowly toward the sound, restrained by the voluminous skirts and petticoats of her Founder's Day costume. She shivered, recalling all the ghost stories that had been told about the shaft directly beneath her.

"Help me!"

It was hard to spot, because of the masses of tissue paper that festooned the area. The boards behind the podium were splintered, leaving an opening into the old shaft.

"Help me, please!"

That was a real voice, not a ghost or the wind. Maria took her long green skirt in hand and balanced precariously at the edge of the ragged wood, looking into the darkness of the old shaft. "Hello! Are you all right? Who are you?"

"Maria?" the voice called in relief. "Maria, is that you?"

It was Ricky Lightner. Maria couldn't believe it.

"Ricky," she asked, "how did you get down there?"

"It was a joke," he answered, a sob catching in his voice. "It was just supposed to be a joke. On the sheriff. He was just supposed to step down on the loose board and catch his foot in the crack. It would've made him look stupid when he gave his speech. Everyone would've laughed. I don't know what happened. The boards gave way when I tried to cut them."

"I'll have to go for help," Maria said, angry at the young man despite her fears for his safety. "Just hold on, Ricky. It'll be all right."

"Don't leave me, Maria! That other boy that died in here—" Ricky cried "—I can feel him down here with me."

"Don't talk like that," Maria pleaded, looking over the applauding crowd and the bright sunshine, wishing she could catch someone's eye without leaving Ricky. "It's going to be okay. You're going to be okay."

The parade was in full formation. Maria watched the Lightner family ride by in their black buggy, waving to the crowd. She tried to get their attention, but the noise from the crowd was too loud. They rode by without knowing their son was trapped in the old shaft.

"Where are you, Joe?" she whispered.

"Maria?" He answered as though he had heard her.

She looked at him, tall and broad-shouldered, dressed all in black with a huge silver star pinned on his chest and a fake mustache on his lip. He was holding a copy of the dedication speech he was going to give after the parade.

"Joe! Ricky's trapped in the old mine shaft! He fell through the boards!"

"Maria?" Ricky called. "Tell the sheriff I'm sorry about the office. Tommy and I did it. I know it was wrong. Tell him I didn't want anyone to get hurt. It was supposed to be a joke."

"You can tell him when they bring you up, Ricky," she told him firmly. "You aren't going to die in there."

"That boy died down here," he answered pitifully.

"But you aren't going to die down there, Ricky," Joe told him in a deep voice as he knelt beside her. "You're going to come up and everything's going to work out. No one's going to let anything happen to you. Stay with him," he said to Maria, touching her arm. "I'll get help."

"Sheriff, I want to make it up to everyone." Ricky started to cry. "I just want to live. I'm sorry."

Maria searched her mind for something to say to Josh's baby brother that would make him feel less frantic. She wasn't sure they could bring him up from the deep shaft.

"Ricky?" She called his name, listening to him sob. "It's going to be all right. The sheriff went for help. They'll be able to pull you right out of there."

"Okay." His voice was muffled by the fifty feet of dirt between him and the surface. "Are they coming yet?"

She looked around but didn't see anyone from the rescue squad or any of the deputies. What if Joe was too late? What if they couldn't help Ricky and he died in the shaft?

"Maria? Are you still there?"

As she started to answer, she saw Joe running back toward her with a coil of rope hanging around his shoulder. E.J. was close behind him, and the flashing lights of the rescue squad drew people's attention.

"They're coming, Ricky," she told him quickly. "They're going to have you out in no time."

There was no room for Maria to stay and talk to Ricky. She moved aside for the rescue workers.

"Somebody's going to have to go down there with the rope," E.J. said with a shake of his head. "He won't be able to tie it around himself."

"Somebody'll have to go headfirst to do that," one of the rescue squad volunteers speculated. "There's not enough room to turn around in that shaft."

"I'll go," Joe said, and he tied the rope around his feet. "Just make sure you pull hard on that rope when I tell you."

E.J. exchanged glances with the other workers. "Count on it, Sheriff."

Maria wanted to ask if there wasn't someone else who could do the job, but she knew the answer before she asked the question. It was part of his life. Part of who he was.

The short time they'd known each other raced through her mind as she watched them lower him into the narrow shaft. She loved him. There had to be some chance for happiness for them if he felt the same.

She didn't regret the life she'd made with Josh. She wouldn't regret the life she'd make with Joe…if she got the opportunity.

"What's happening?" Tommy demanded from the scaffolding.

"Ricky is trapped in the shaft," Maria told him bluntly, wanting to tell him that he was to blame.

"What?" Anna Lightner demanded from behind him.

Maria sighed and turned to face her. "He said it was supposed to be a joke on the sheriff. He wanted to make a spot big enough in the platform so Joe would step in and catch his foot when he stepped up to the platform. He didn't realize what he was doing.''

"How far is he in?'' Joel asked softly.

Maria shrugged. "Maybe fifty feet.''

"Who's up there?'' Tommy started to push past her.

"The sheriff,'' she replied unsteadily. "They're lowering him into the shaft by his feet so he can tie the rope around Ricky.''

"The sheriff?'' Joel Lightner shook his head and looked pointedly at his wife, who'd gone white to her lips.

"I want to know what's going on,'' Tommy said, trying to make his way to the top.

"Stop right there, Tommy,'' Billy said seriously. He was a new deputy, serving for the first time on Founder's Day. "We're doing what we can for Ricky. There isn't enough room for anyone else up here.''

Tommy became subdued after that, standing with his parents. His arm supported his mother's slender waist.

"He told me that the two of you trashed the sheriff's office,'' Maria told Tommy. "He was afraid he was going to die.''

Anna Lightner shuddered and hid her face in her husband's coat. "I can't lose another son,'' she sobbed. "I just can't—''

"Little fool,'' Tommy said, rubbing the back of his neck in his high-collared wool costume.

"He thought he could do whatever he wanted,'' his father explained, glancing at Tommy. "Like you. And we didn't tell him any better. We let him think—''

"We're pulling the sheriff up,'' E.J. yelled down the slope. "He's got the rope tied to Ricky.''

"Oh, please, God,'' Anna cried.

Maria tried to see Joe's face through the crowd of rescue workers. She could barely make out his dirty costume and smudged face. Half of Joe's white shirt was scratched away by the rusted metalwork that lined the old shaft. She wanted to run to him and throw her arms around him and hold him tight. She wanted to tell him she loved him and that she never wanted to come home to a house without him in it again.

"Let's pull him up," Joe said to the men around him.

"You okay?" E.J. asked him, seeing a long, bloody gouge down his side.

"I will be if we can get him out of there," Joe assured him. "The shaft narrowed as it went down, so I can only hope the rope will hold well enough to get Ricky where we can reach him."

Together, they began the process of inching the wedged teenager from the shaft, careful not to dislodge the rope around him. Muscles ached, tendons strained. The warm sun beat down on them all. The crowds gathered, wondering if the whole thing was part of the Founder's Day activities.

Maria prayed with her in-laws, even though her heart beat with the surety of Joe's safety. The irony of him throwing himself down that shaft after Ricky wasn't lost on her. She hoped it wasn't lost on Ricky's family, either.

"I see his face," someone yelled from the lip of the shaft. "He's looking up!"

Sporadic applause greeted his emergence into the sunlight. He was shaken and covered with filth. He lifted his tearstained face to the blue sky, and the crowd went wild.

"He's all right!" Joel Lightner yelled, raising his wife's head. "He's all right!"

Deputies ringed the excavation, keeping the crowd from the area where the rescue workers were trying to get the boy in place to transport him to the nearest hospital.

They finally carried Ricky down the hill on a stretcher, his neck in a brace. He was cheered by a throng of well-wishers. His mother and father wordlessly accompanied their son, looking suddenly fragile and older than they had earlier in the day.

"How is he?" Maria asked as Joe reached her. His face was dirty and a little scratched, but he looked like life and love to her.

"He'll be okay," Joe said, noticing Tommy standing at Maria's side. "Maybe a couple of broken ribs from the fall. Probably nothing serious."

"You saved my brother's life," Tommy muttered, staring at Joe as though he'd never seen him before.

"That's my job," Joe returned, not backing down from Tommy's regard.

E.J. came up beside them. "Tommy, you'd better come with me. There's going to be some questions to answer about the vandalism at the sheriff's office."

"Ricky didn't know what he was saying," Tommy argued.

"All the same," E.J. continued, "let's make this easy, huh?"

Tommy looked at Maria. "I don't have anything to say."

E.J. shrugged, taking his arm. "I think we should wait in the new jail, then, until you can get your lawyer down here."

People were still clustered around the shaft and the

podium, asking questions and looking at the new sheriff.

Joe excused himself from Maria's side and stepped to the podium, carefully avoiding the gaping hole. He hoped never to see the inside of a mine shaft again.

"I don't think we're going to be dedicating this shaft today," he said, taking off the fake mustache with a careless hand. "So, if everyone could move down the hill, we'll close off the area then open the park."

He told them Ricky Lightner was going to be fine, and then he urged them to have a good time.

The crowd cheered around Maria, her eyes wet with tears as she listened to him. Hadn't she known he was a hero when she first met him? Suddenly, that didn't seem so bad.

He waded through the crowd toward her amidst good wishes and hearty slaps on the back.

Maria walked beside him to the main street. The deputies were clearing the area and closing the tragic site again, much as they had a hundred years ago, after the first accident.

"Well, that was exciting," Joe said, hoping Maria's worst fears hadn't been realized. "You didn't tell me Founder's Day was full of surprises."

"Surprises?" Maria yelled, turning on him quickly. Without warning, she threw herself against him, kissing him through the mud and slime.

"What the hell was that?" he demanded, holding her close.

"I love you, Joe Roberts! I thought I'd lost you!" She kissed him again, and for a few long moments, the crowd and the dark mine shaft were lost to them.

"Maria," he said finally, seriously, looking at her

beautiful face in the sunshine. "I don't think I can give up what I do. I love you and I'll try to be careful—"

"I wouldn't ask you to give it up," she promised. "Just come home to me every night."

Joe kissed her, leaving a smear of dirt from his cheek on her chin. "It won't always be easy. I'm not Josh. But if we love each other enough and we're willing to give it a chance, we can make it work out."

"I do love you," she answered, wrapping her arms around him and hugging him tightly to her. "And you aren't Josh. But you are a hero."

"I can work with that," he replied fiercely, crushing her to him. "I want to help make a life for you and Sam."

"And Rachel?" she whispered against his throat.

"I loved Rachel. And I've grieved for her. I've lived alone with that mistake in my record and my soul for the past fifteen years."

"But not any longer," she said, kissing him quickly. "Not by yourself."

"Not by myself," he agreed, loving her with his eyes. "I like the sound of that."

Epilogue

They waited anxiously for the returns, exchanging smiles across the crowded room, trying to assure one another that whatever the outcome, they would still be all right.

Maria felt an ache beginning in her lower back and knew she should sit down, but she was too full of excitement and impatience to do anything except pace. The baby was kicking restlessly within her, but the birth was several months away.

Sam didn't understand. When he'd heard he was going to have a baby brother or sister, he was anxious to begin that new life at once. To a ten-year-old, nine months was forever.

In the two years Maria and Joe had been married, they had built a new life together. A wonderful house had been found, mysteriously, by the Lightner family, and donated to the new sheriff.

Tommy and Ricky Lightner had done some community service work after being convicted of harassment and malicious destruction. The Lightner family had encouraged Tommy to take a logging job in the Pacific Northwest after it was over.

The town of Gold Springs had made a place in their hearts for their new sheriff. All that was left was the rest of the county.

It was getting late. Joe watched Maria rub her lower back another time, then crossed the room toward her, intent on insisting she sit down and rest.

There was a new warmth in him that he cherished and feared. After being married and having Sam and Maria in his life, Joe could understand her initial reluctance to becoming involved with him. But he thanked God every day that she had taken a chance on him.

"Sheriff!" someone yelled from across the noisy room. There were calls for quiet as the announcer on the television screen began to tally the election finals.

Joe reached Maria's side and wrapped an arm around her waist, liking the way she leaned against him, beginning to think of other things they could be doing besides waiting for election returns.

"And for sheriff of Chatner County, the votes have been tabulated, and incumbent Joseph Roberts has taken the spot for another six years."

A shout went up from the crowd of supporters. Billy, E.J. and other deputies gathered around to shake his hand and congratulate him. Joe said a few words, and there were cheers and much throwing of confetti.

"Let's go home," Joe whispered in Maria's ear.

She looked at him. "Can we do that?"

"I think you need to be home...in bed. What do you think?"

"I know where the back door is, Sheriff," she replied with a loving smile.

"Where you go…" he promised, wondering how he had lived without her. "I love you, Maria."

"I love you." She kissed him quickly then grabbed his hand. "Let's go."

*   *   *   *   *

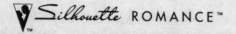

If you enjoyed what you just read,
then we've got an offer you can't resist!

Take 2 bestselling love stories FREE!

Plus get a FREE surprise gift!

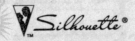

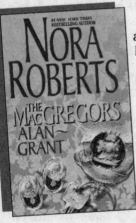

Based on the bestselling miniseries

A FORTUNE'S CHILDREN *Wedding:*
THE HOODWINKED BRIDE

by BARBARA BOSWELL

This March, the Fortune family discovers a twenty-six-year-old secret—beautiful Angelica Carroll *Fortune!* Kate Fortune hires Flynt Corrigan to protect the newest Fortune, and this jaded investigator soon finds this his most tantalizing—and tormenting—assignment to date....

Barbara Boswell's single title is just one of the captivating romances in Silhouette's exciting new miniseries, **Fortune's Children: The Brides,** featuring six special women who perpetuate a family legacy that is greater than mere riches!

Look for *The Honor Bound Groom,* by Jennifer Greene, when **Fortune's Children: The Brides** launches in Silhouette Desire in January 1999!

Available at your favorite retail outlet.

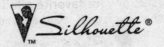

World's Most Eligible Bachelors

**Available March 1999 from
Silhouette Books...**

Doctor in Disguise
by Gina Wilkins

The World's Most Eligible Bachelor: Tall, dark and devastating Dr. Alex Keating's cure for his chronic bachelorhood: "Take" sexy Carly Fletcher and call her in the morning!

One bump to the head left Dr. Alex Keating stranded in the tender loving care of down-home physician Carly Fletcher. She knew nothing of his stellar credentials, but his long, lean physique and seductive smile were all she *needed* to know to write this stubborn patient a prescription for love!

Each month, Silhouette Books brings you a brand-new story about an absolutely irresistible bachelor. Find out how the sexiest, most sought-after men are finally caught.

Available at your favorite retail outlet.

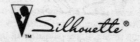

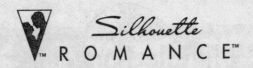

COMING NEXT MONTH

#1354 HUSBAND FROM 9 TO 5—Susan Meier
Loving the Boss
For days, Molly Doyle had thought she was Mrs. Jack Cavanaugh, and Jack played along—then she got her memory back, and realized she was only his *secretary*. So how could she convince her bachelor boss to make their pretend marriage real?

#1355 CALLAGHAN'S BRIDE—Diana Palmer
Virgin Brides Anniversary/Long Tall Texans
Callaghan Hart exasperated temporary ranch cook Tess Brady by refusing to admit that the attraction they shared was more than just passion. Could Tess make Callaghan see she was his truelove bride before her time on the Hart Ranch ran out?

#1356 A RING FOR CINDERELLA—Judy Christenberry
The Lucky Charm Sisters
The last thing Susan Greenwood expected when she went into her family's diner was a marriage proposal! But cowboy Zack Lowery was in desperate need of a fiancée to fulfill his grandfather's dying wish. Still, she was astonished at the power of pretense when *acting* in love started to feel a lot like *being* in love!

#1357 TEXAS BRIDE—Kate Thomas
Charming lawyer Josh Walker had always wanted a child. So when the woman who saved him from a car wreck went into labor, he was eager to care for her and her son. Yet lazy days—and nights—together soon had Josh wanting to make Dani *his*...forever!

#1358 SOLDIER AND THE SOCIETY GIRL—Vivian Leiber
He's My Hero
Refined protocol specialist Chessy Banks Bailey had thirty days to transform rough 'n' rugged, true-grit soldier Derek McKenna into a polished spokesman. Her mission seemed quite impossible...until lessons in etiquette suddenly turned into lessons in love....

#1359 SHERIFF TAKES A BRIDE—Gayle Kaye
Family Matters
Hallie Cates didn't pay much attention to the new sheriff in town—until Cam Osborne arrested her grandmother for moonshining! Hallie swore to prove her grandmother's innocence. But she was soon caught up in the strong, passionate arms of the law herself!